The Wrenchies

Farel Dalrymple

First Second
New York

the wrenchies
72

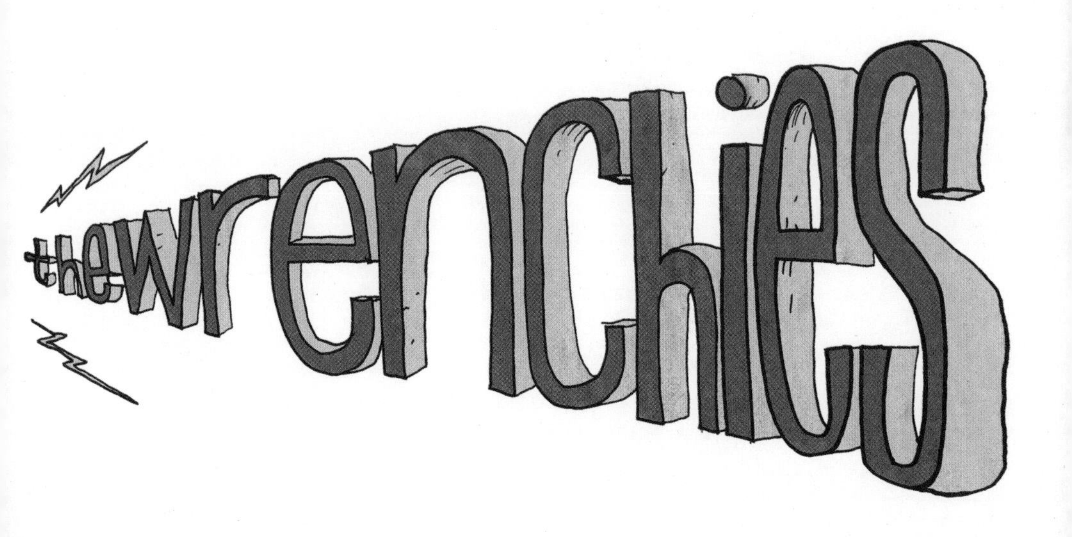
thewrenchies

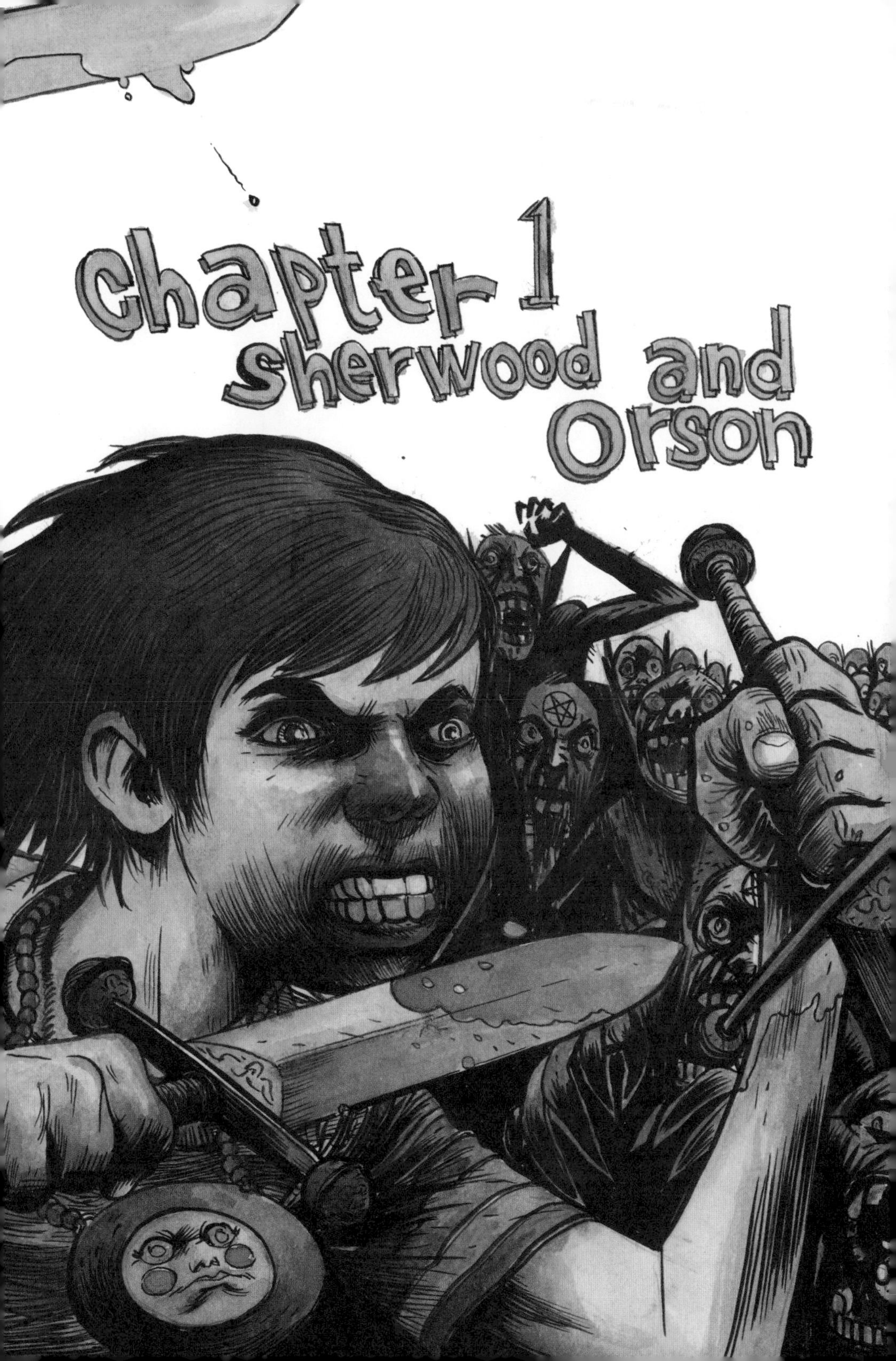
Chapter 1
Sherwood and Orson

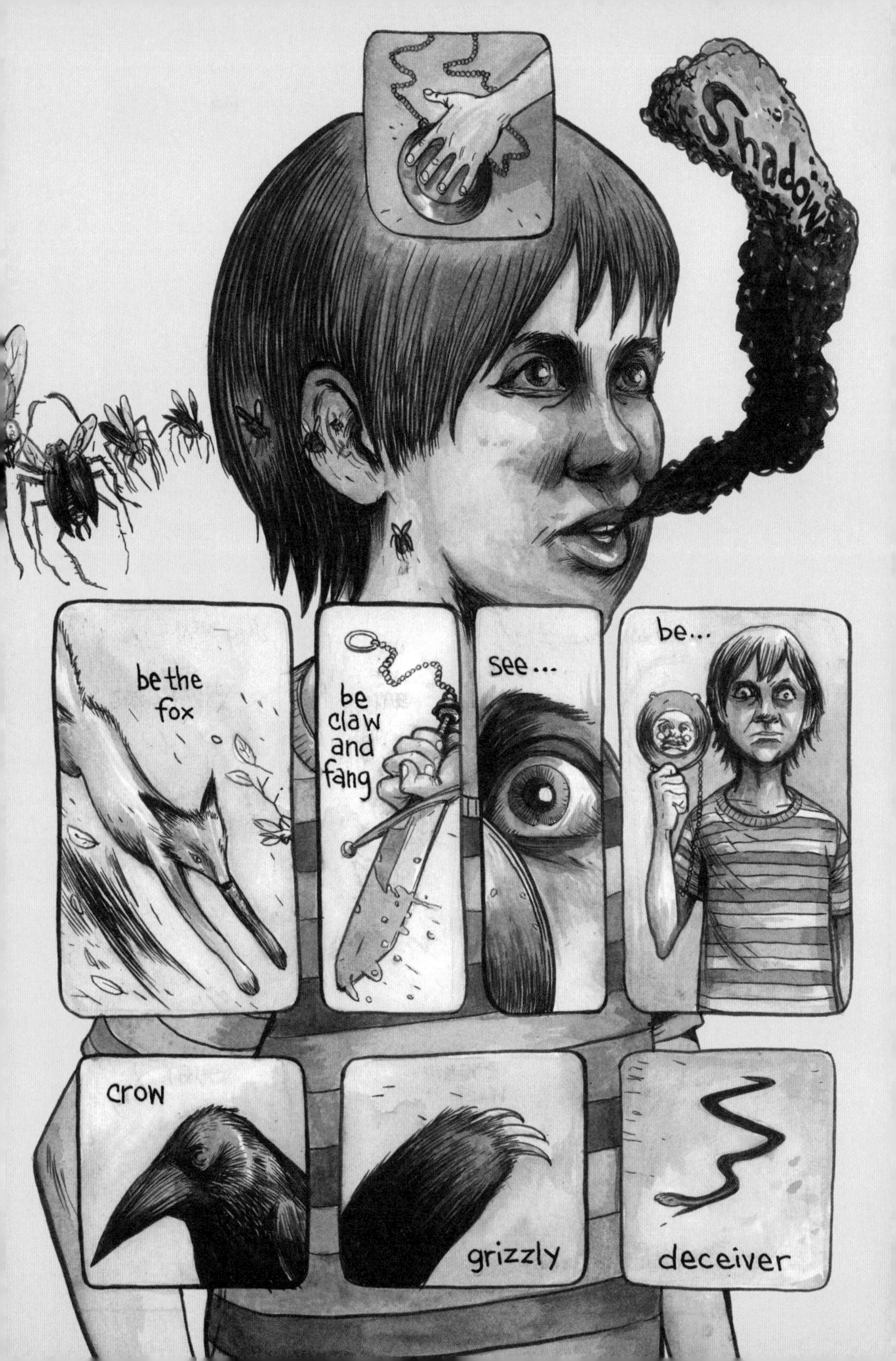
Shadow...
be the fox
be claw and fang
see...
be...
crow
grizzly
deceiver

That day my brother and I faced our first demon.

That day...
we began our
long journey through
an insidious and
profane realm.
Innocence
dissolved quickly
after we
stepped
into...
the cave.

WOOD sinner CAV

The cave
changed us.

made us.

The cave
cost us.

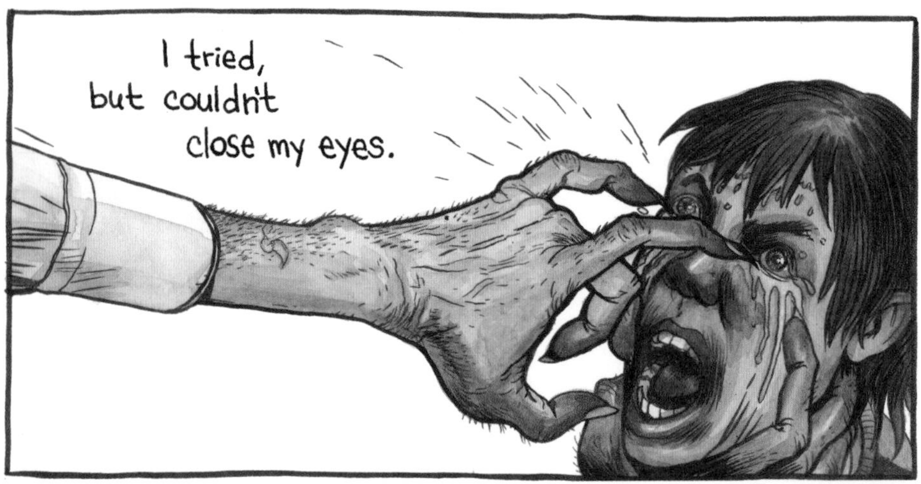
I tried,
but couldn't
close my eyes.

We weren't supposed to go in there.

We never should have entered the shadows.

Something left a back door open.

THE OLDEST FIRST!
Sherwood Presley Breadcoat
Acquiring knowledge.
Sacred wisdom.
cripes!

I wanted to barf, and I think I was screaming a lot.

Mostly though I remember listening to the voice of that thing at my feet.

It was singing to me.

Then something
screamed inside my head.

WOW.
my eyes...
my guts...
they burned.

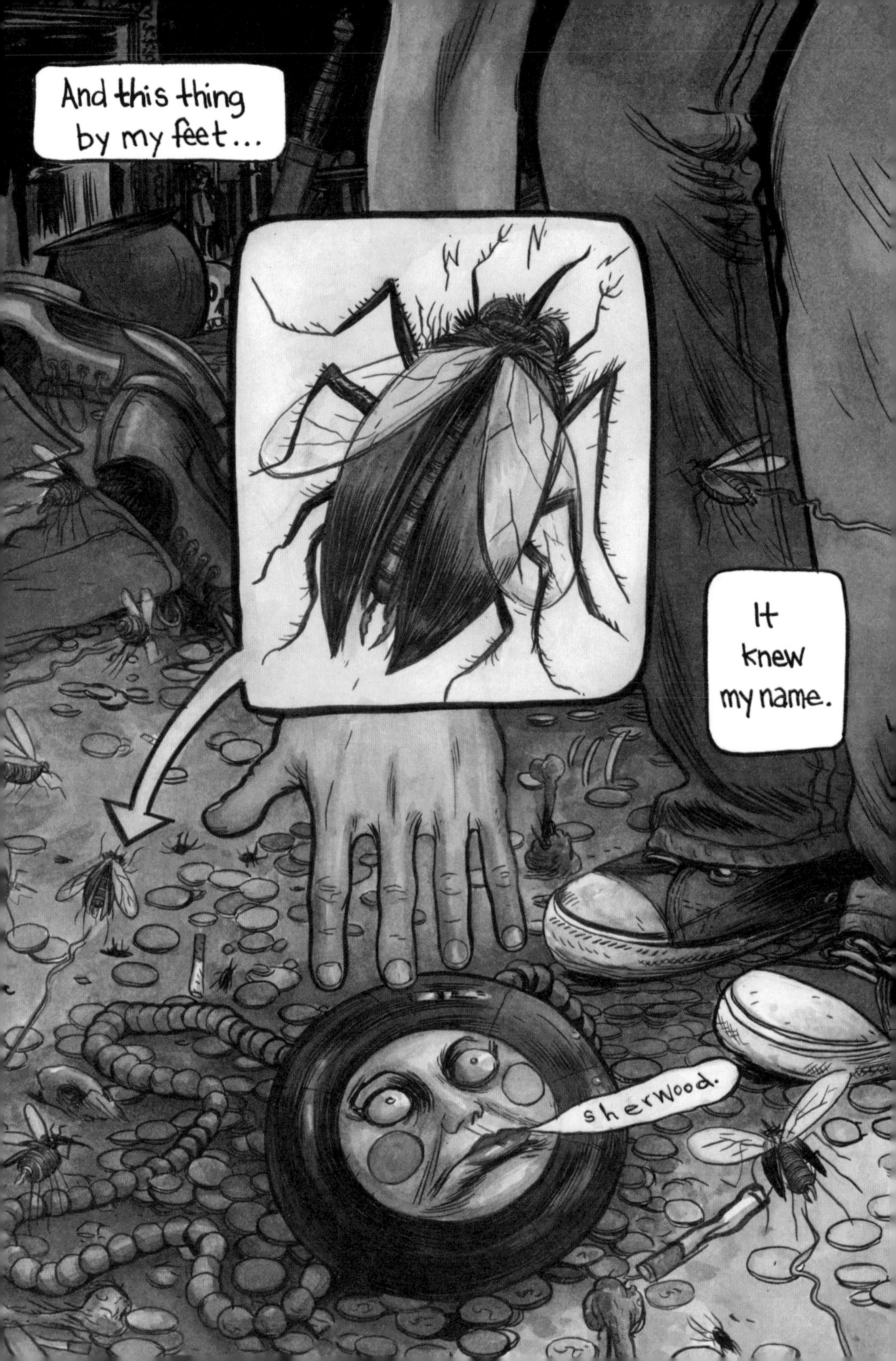
And this thing by my feet...
It knew my name.
sherwood.

are you ok?

sherwood?

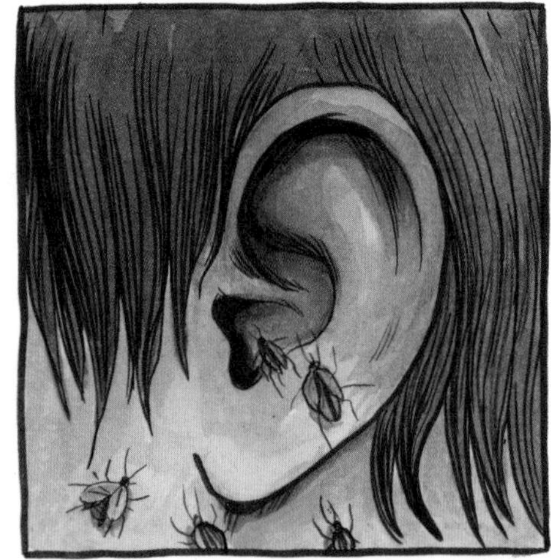

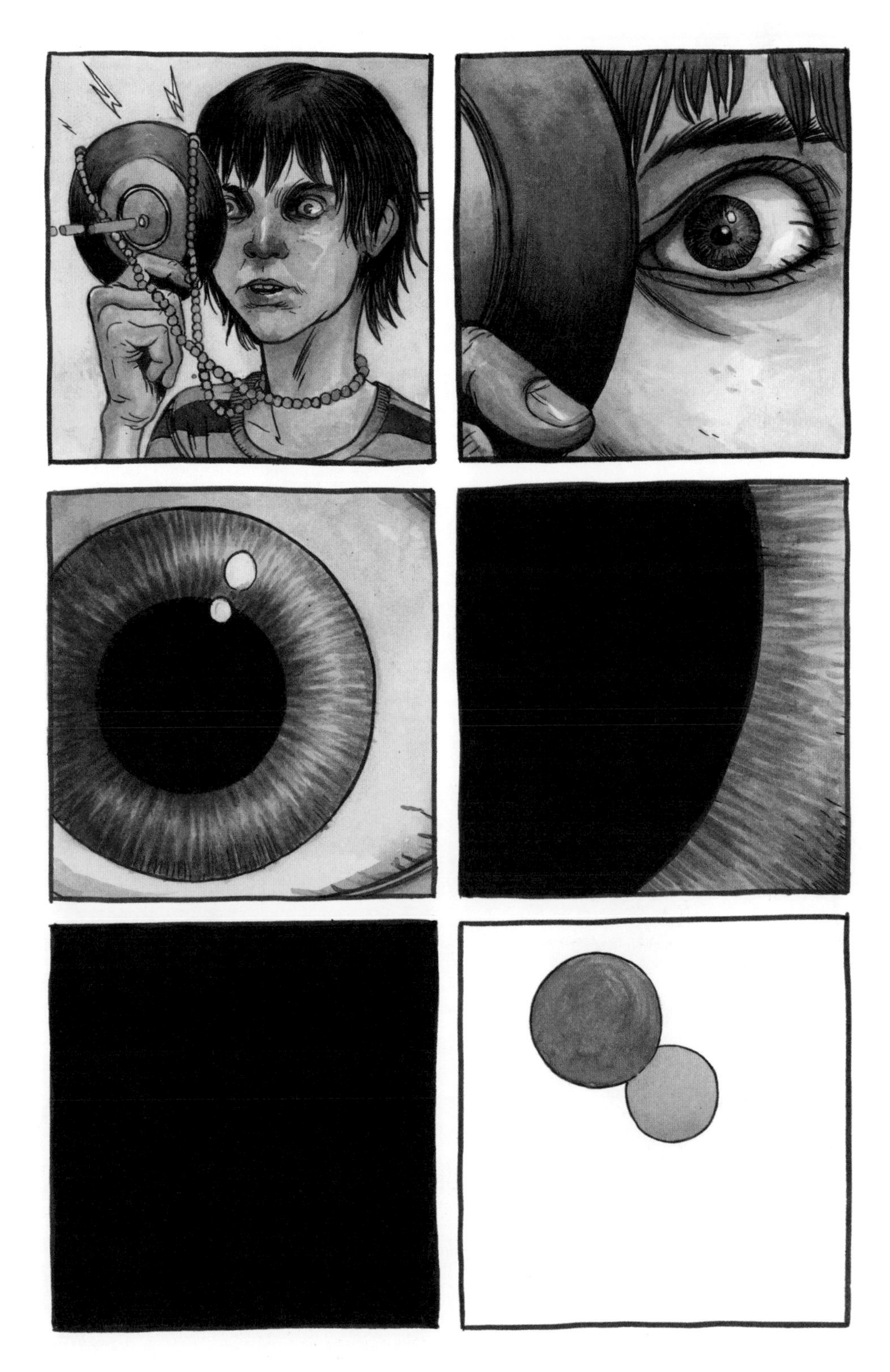

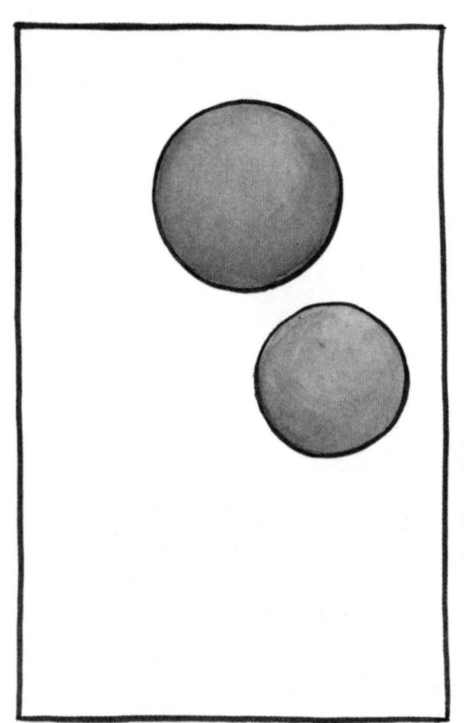

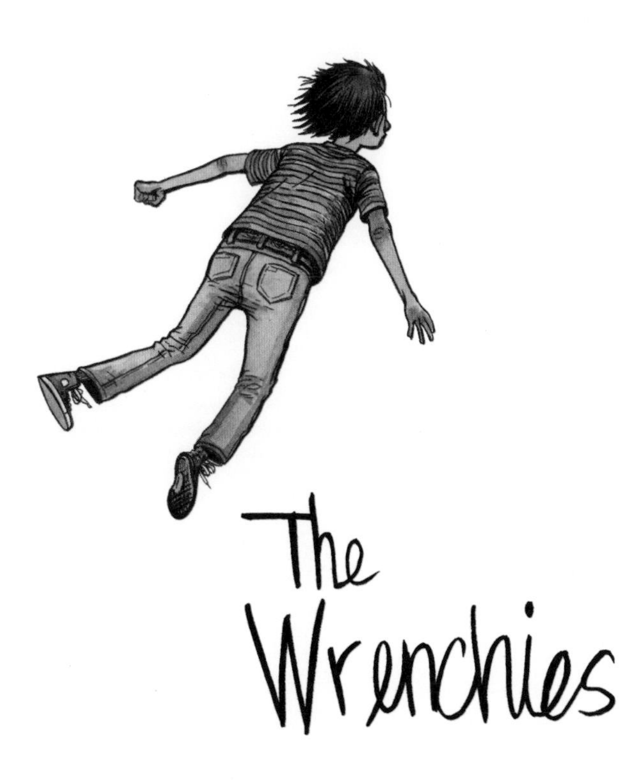
The
Wrenchies

Chapter 2
the young Wrenchies

Tad
Bance
Jad

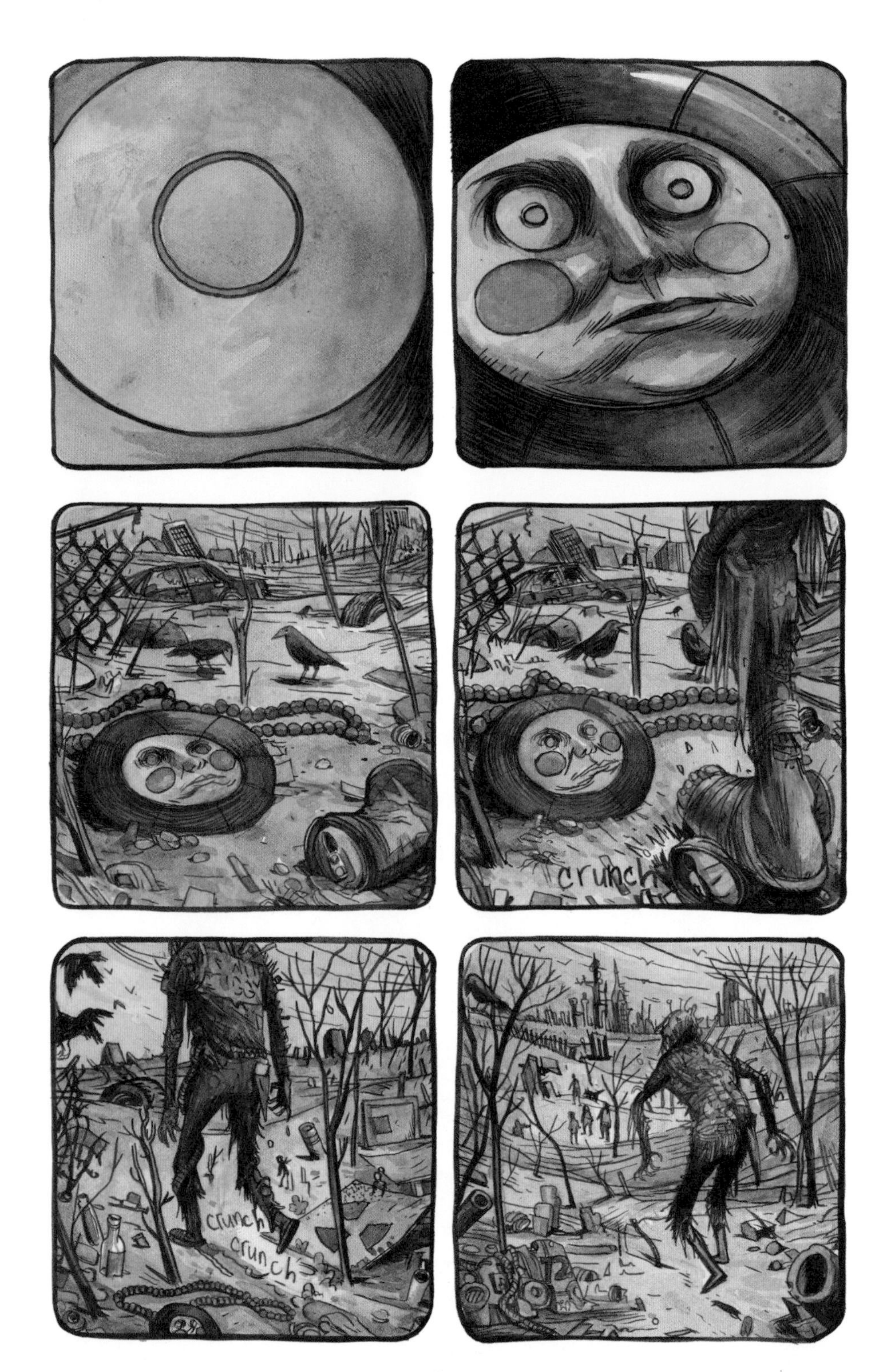
crunch
crunch
crunch

th-th-th-th - th

Wow, Tad, how'd you learn to do that?
I didn't think that weapon even worked.

hrmmm

I want to shoot something, too.
I'll look for a gun for you, Marsi.
Look at all these stinky little pixie things.

Tad modified that himself. My brother is a genius with that ancient shit.

What did you find, Tad?
Hey, It's a comic book.

Comic book?
cool.

The Wrenchies? That's the name of OUR gang.
Yeah, that's where I got the name from.
You've never seen that comic before?

snif snif

I don't know if I've ever seen ANY comic book before. It looks really weird.
Well, they're not for every-body.
~skruntch.
stuff
comics shmomix
Look for shit we can use.
Yeah, demons might be here soon.
snif
I wonder if that gun could hurt THEM.
snif
snif
hrrr mm

Someone out there, Murmur? Zombies? Vampires?
rrrrr

Oh, it's just them,

The Zekes!

Hey, Shakey.
Jad.
You guys find anything today?

Skrank smells some goods.
What is that behind your back, Tad?
hissssss

The Wrenchies issue one.
The Wrenchies

You should let me check that out, man.

Back off, Shakey!
I could take it to my older sister. She used to read loads of those things.

Don't try using your magic spheres on us.
Yeah, we know what's up.
Don't make us kick your ass again, wizard.
Whatever. It's just a dumb comic book. keep it.
There's better, cooler stuff out here in the piles.
But...
If it WAS worth it to me we could take what I wanted from you ...
growr.
anytime I wanted.
Yeah, try it.
rrrrr

Yeah, just shut your mutt up. He's way too jumpy.

rrrr rrr

What is it, Murmur?

What do you see?

DON'T LET THEM TOUCH AND DESPAIR YOU!

HA!

THESE GUYS ARE WIMPS!

yeah.

SSShhh.
grk.

NNNooooo
hisss

NOOOOOOoooooo

urk
urk

HEY! WATCH IT!

DON'T LET THEM GET TO YOU.
YOU'D BE LIKE THEM.
I know.

Think happy thoughts.

You're welcome, Wizard.
THANKS!

SHAKEY! STOP! Look at its forehead. It's got the mark.
?

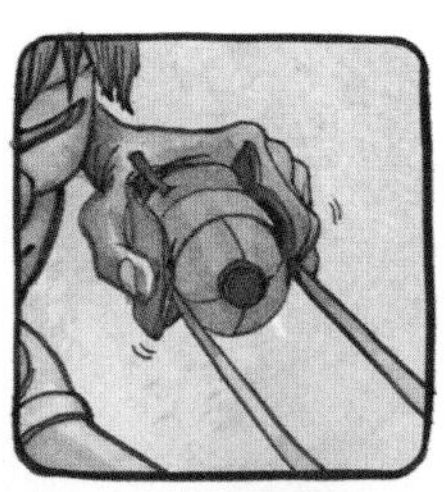

IF YOU KILL THAT KIND THE SHADOWSMEN WILL KNOW!
THEY'LL COME FOR US ALL!
meh.
Zerm's dead anyway.

ha.
Great Shot.
WOW Tad, you really nailed it.
Stupid kid, now we're all doomed.
THAT WAS A DEMON WIZARD YOU JUST SMOKED, MAN!
We don't give a damn. Tad hates Wizards...

None of us much care for WIZARDS.

You were gonna let that THING take your own man down THERE.
ZERM WAS THE SAME AS DEAD.

YOU'D LET ONE OF YOUR OWN CREW BECOME A NIGHTMARE,

YEAH, WELL YOUR BOY JUST BROUGHT SHADOWSMEN DOWN ON ALL OF US!

Psssh, we all know you had to give up part of your soul to use those magic spheres.

So that's why you're scared, you're already tied to the Shadowsmen.

We aren't afraid of the Shadowsmen, zombies, demons, or wizards.

That's dumb. Once we get old enough they are gonna get us all anyway.
Yeah.

We will fight.
We will escape.
They will not take us.
So dramatic.
Yeah, let those demons come and try to turn me into one of them.
NOT ME, MAN!
No way.
The Shadowsmen and their kind are truly and completely evil, but we don't need to give in to fear.
See how fast THEY Disintegrate?
See how they Dissolve.

Returnin to Wher they came from.
I hope someday all the garbage that covers the earth dissolves just like that.
Stoney's real good with words.

The trash reclaims their bodies.

You guys are all nuts, but I got to admire that.

I hope all of you die.

yeah,
We ARE the best.

HELL

overseers

AREA 72

In this doom only children come and go listening to illegal radios.

THE NON ZOMBIES
STAY AWAY!

Uh, Bance, What the hell is THAT?

I've seen it before.
Just wandering the wastes, like it's looking for something...
...or someone.

AARRRRRRRRRRGH!
ahem.

French ♫ penitentiary system, it must have-
have cost a ♩ fortune ♫
THE EMPTY TRAIN IS BURNING ♫ YOUR SINFUL BRAIN ♫
THIS EMPTY ♫ CAR IS DIGGING YOUR GAME.
Whoah.
FRANK LLOYD WRIGHT'S butler ♫ hacked them into some pieces, ♫ I hacked them into some bits. ♫

ARE YOU OK?
I don't think... OH MAN. I... IT'S JUST THAT I ATE A BUNCH OF PILLS...

BUT I THINK I POPPED A RED BY MISTAKE. I'M GONNA GO LIE DOWN AT THE CLUBHOUSE.
I THINK I'M GONNA GO TOO.

This band kind of sucks anyway.
LATER, FELLAS.
bye

SO THEN THIS KID COMES BACK INTO THE BUILDING...
Do you have any more of those pills?

THEN BODES, he lives there, WENT TOTAL PSYCHO ON HIM.
HE RUNS RIGHT UP TO THE KID AND THROWS A HEADLOCK ON HIM.

THEN BODES DRAGS THIS KID OUTSIDE AND THEY BOTH FALL DOWN, RIGHT DOWN IN THE SNOW!
AS SOON AS THEY HIT THE GROUND BODES PUTS HIS MOUTH RIGHT ON THE KID'S EAR and YELLS!

AND I MEAN HE IS YELLLLL-ING! He still has the kid in a headlock and they were splayed out on the ground, and fucking Bodesy was SCREAMING probably as loud as he could get, right into that punk's ear!

I'm sure that kid went deaf in that ear. HA! I can still remember him stumbling away holding his GODDAMN EAR. I MEAN FUCKIN' BRUTAL, RIGHT?

IT'S WEIRD HOW THAT GUY BODES ALWAYS KNOWS THE PERFECT THING TO DO.
?

THAT DUDE is fucked up though, man. Yeah.

Hey, wait up.

PAPER WENT FLYING THROUGH THE EMPTY ELEVATOR SHAFT.

A GHOST WANDERED THROUGH THE CORRIDORS

HEY Griener!

What are you PISSING and spazzing about now?
HEY!
We saw you Wrenchies talking to the Zekes gang to-

You're gonna see the light, Greiner.

You better be cautious, Bance.
Think about what you say.
ha.

You are an ugly an' stupid jerk.
Holy hell, B. Those insults sucked.
Be cool. Fortune.

Thanks. I'm gonna get—

this.

oooooofff
grrk
Geeze, Bance.
holy crap.
Yeah, Yeah.
He owed me this.

YOU KILLED HIM!
Yeah, I'm taking his sticks too.

HOW COULD YOU?!
ONE OF US!?

He wasn't really one of us.
The night creeps were using him.
See for yourself. He was wrong.

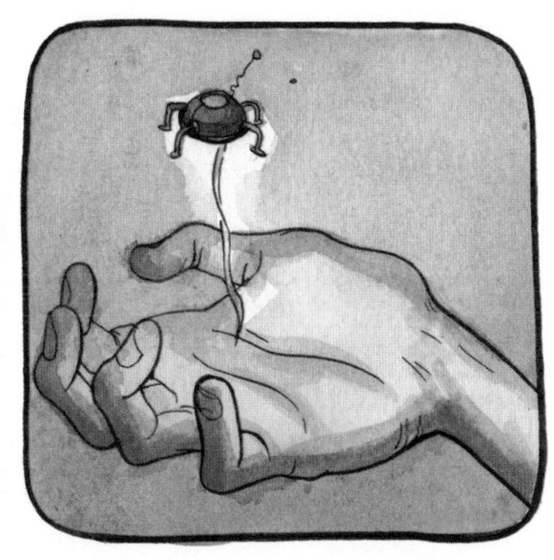

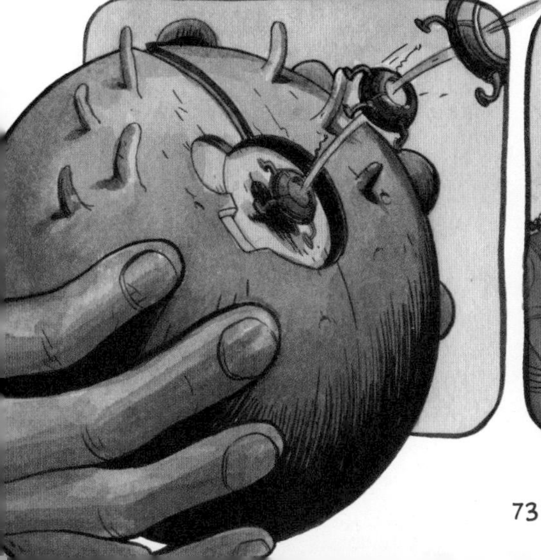

...
the dark was in him.

I can see it now.

HA HAHA

Something's bugging me.
No SHIT.
Some strange feeling since this morning...

...Hey Tad, can I check out that Wrenchies comic?

There is something in this book, I know it.
I'm just not smart enough to figure out what it is.
The Wrenchies

I remember first seeing this comic when I was a little kid.
What could it mean?
The Wrenchies

WHAT'S YOUR DEAL WITH THAT BOOK ANYWAY?
I don't know... I feel like it is trying to tell me something...
The Wrenchies
skratch skratch

Does that sound weird?
WHY DON'T WE ASK SHAKEY'S SISTER?

So, You guys are currently the hot shit gang or whatever.
Don't you hang out with my little brother?
burp
pervert
nom
ba

yep.
yeah.
You SEEN THIS?

Oh yeah. heh.
I used to have a ton of comics.

This one kind of sucks.
But there is some-thing...

When I was younger I could see some sort of hidden message all up and through the pages, hidden inside the panels...

But I can't see it anymore.
The Wrenchies

You should talk to Shakey's friend, Olweyez.
Where is Shakey?

How should I know? Just `cause that dork is related to me doesn't mean that I babysit him.
Ok! Geeze.

But that Olweyez guy lives on the East side, near the old Stag. In some trash hole.

Ok, let's have that back now.
I can't even remember now why I was so into those.
The Wrenchies

Anyway, I suppose I don't need anything where I'm going.

Hey, ask them if they got any pink ones.
CAN IT, BAGS!
Let's get going, man.
here ya go, Tad.

Man, Nom got so drunk last night he started ripping shit off the walls and screaming, "We're all already dead!"
yeah.
THEY'RE SHORT. YOU CAN TELL.

Yeah, Night Creeps will be coming for them soon.
BAGS

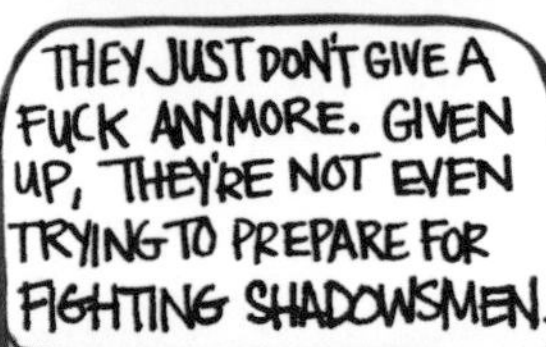
THEY JUST DON'T GIVE A FUCK ANYMORE. GIVEN UP, THEY'RE NOT EVEN TRYING TO PREPARE FOR FIGHTING SHADOWSMEN.

pervert
No way the creeps are takin' us when we come of age! No way in hell!

YEAH. WHAT A BUNCH OF LOSERS, THOUGH.
Yeah, it's sad.
NOM
SABINA'S ALL RIGHT, BUT HER CREW... SHE SHOULD DUMP THOSE FOOLS AND RUN.

They were great fighters once though. Even though they stink like shit now.
Someone please remember us.
stanly spuitt
NO KIDDING. THEY ALL SMELL PRETTY DAMN RANK.

Fuck this place, man. This world is such a bad place.
All rotten and decayed!

It's all shit!

BE COOL, BANCE! LOOK AT WHO JUST SHOWED UP.

IT COULD BE A DRAG TO ATTRACT THAT SORT OF ATTENTION RIGHT NOW.

NIGHT CREEPS!
hissssssss

ONCE WE'RE OUT-SIDE, WE SPLIT UP, OK?
IF YOU'RE FOLLOWED USE ROUTE 72, PLAN 72.
yeah

no.
HEY!
What the hell?

GO!
help us.
SHADOWS-MEN!

So the creeps bust up another lame party. You know, Belf, I am getting sick of all this bullshit. Not just the Shadowsmen, but this whole stupid party scene.
I get you there. I'm pretty tired of it all as well.
I'll be talking to someone, then just lose myself in thought about what an asshole and weirdo I am.
HA! Yeah, then you realize that you have no idea of what was being said by whoever was talking.
fucking bad guys!

Hey, this punch is GOOD!
Yeah, like that and all the other awkward moments.
All the bullshit conversations.
All the repeated Jokes.
Not your own of course.
Of course not.
I swear to myself I'm not ever going out, but then I eventually do the same shit again.
And then repeat.

help.

ONE WAY

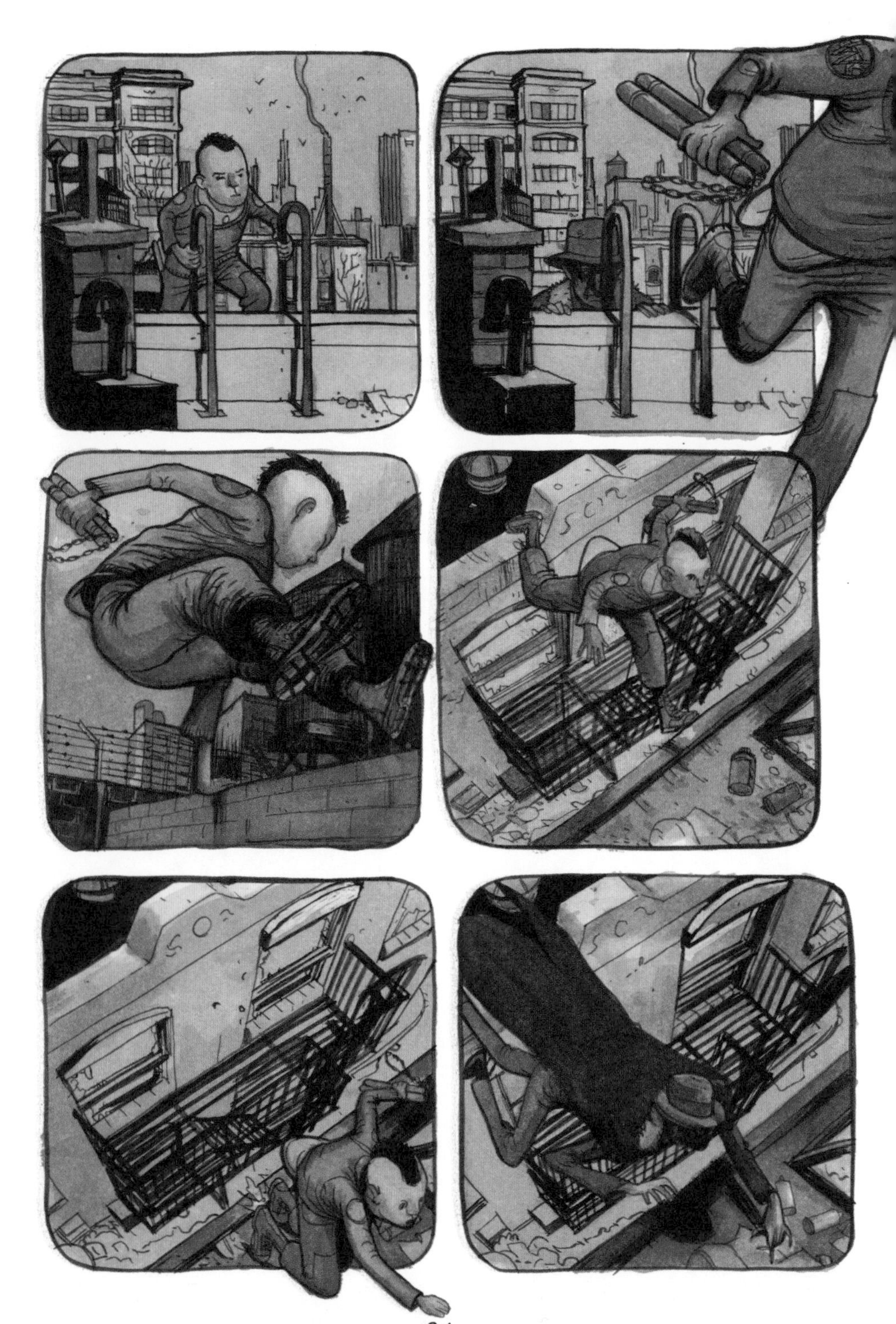

You don't scare me, demon.

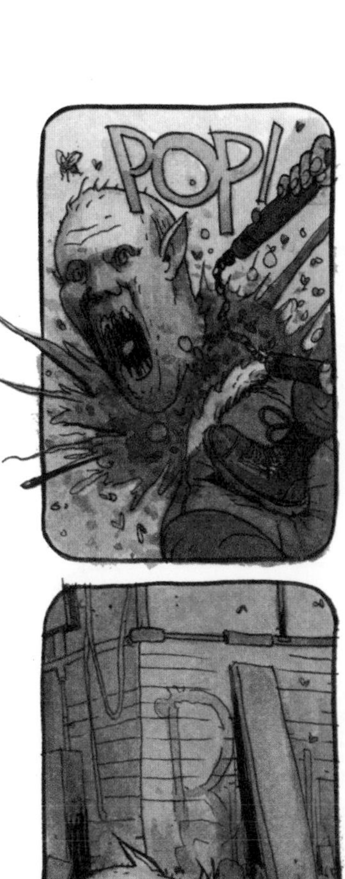
POP!

bonk
BONK

pSSSSS

hey, bug.

This is Wrenchies turf.
SPLAT
squish

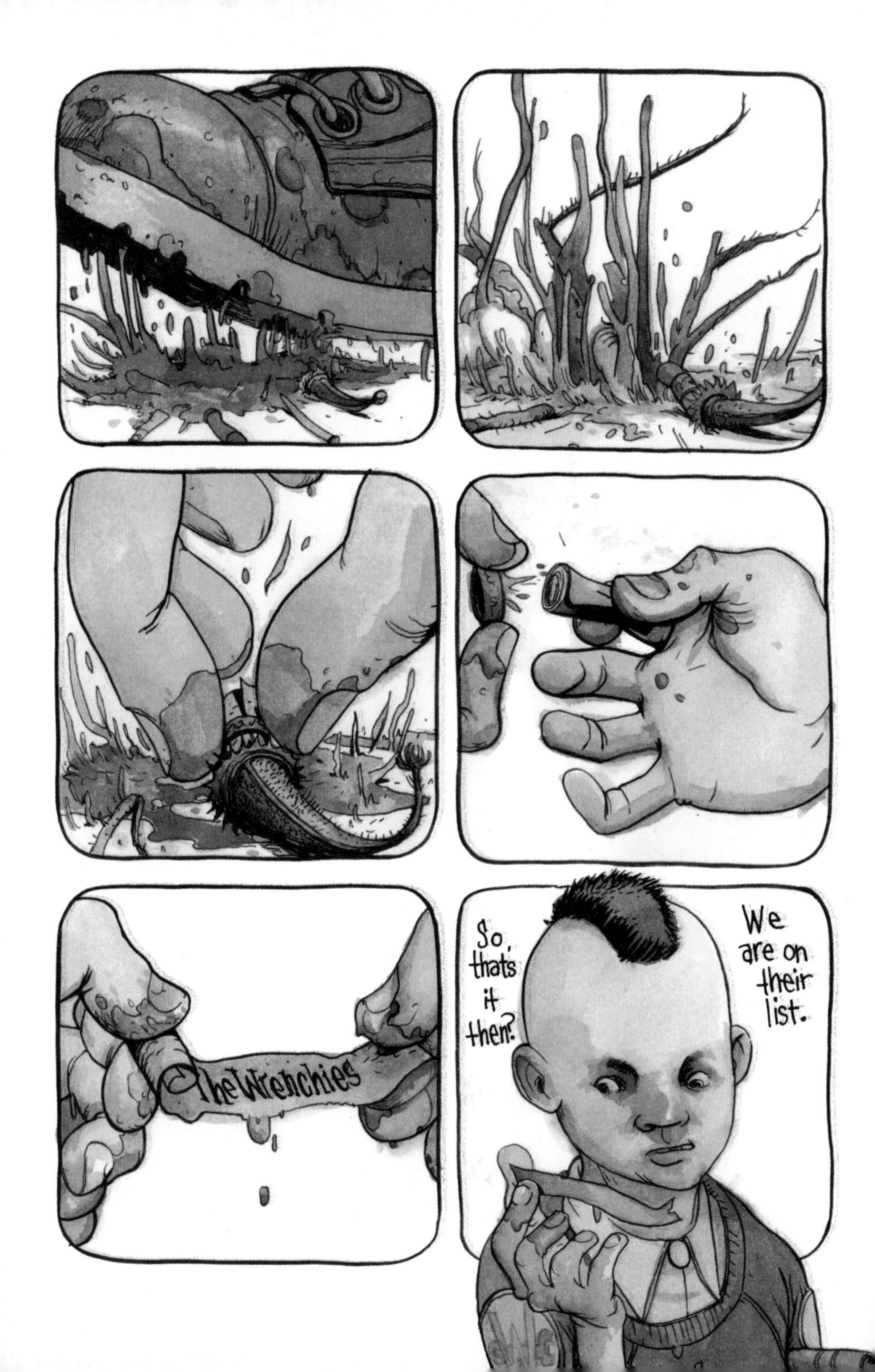
The Wrenchies
So that's it then?
We are on their list.

Melt away, you freak face.
When is the last time I used this entrance?

the Witchlings' secret underground base, protected by ancient magic.
POP
pop
What's with all the dudes in here?
c'mon lemme out.

Heeey, Bance!
We heard you guys had trouble.
!

Nah, no trouble.
aw, c'mon.

Tad and I ambushed our creep with that boobytrap in the sewer. ha!
POP POP!
That ain't loud enough. Ya don't need those ear things.

man, I'd loved to have seen that.
yeah.

ARMORY
retract
chew chew chew

Hey, can I have a bite, Tad?
How did ya do, Bance?
POP POP
eat my shit

So I got this off my creep.

oh.
wow
heh heh
HA.
About time I guess.

HAW HAW
You SUCK!
OH Shit! ha ha ha ha I really cut the fuck out of my hand.

ALL RIGHT KIDS!!!
IF YOU AIN'T GOT A "W" ON YOUR SHOULDER
GET THE HELL OUT!
NOW!

'Night fellas.
'sup B.
That blade was sharp.
kof kof Oi, I am beat man.
mumble
Thanks for letting us crash here.
I'm taking this book to bed.
None of these poor dopes are gonna make it.
Yeah, thanks guys,
Lots of creeps out tonight.

Sorry, Bance, the Ziade gang just sort of followed me here.
S'cool, Fortune. I'm just real tired is all.
Great job kicking ass tonight, by the way.
rub rub

HAHA Stoney is still trippin' balls.
yeeahh...
But the drugs ARE helping me see all sorts of things in this comic book.
chew
WoW.

I am jealous of Stoney's confidence with drugs.
We really ought to all get to bed though...
Yep, it's like her best super power. she can handle all of them.
It all makes sense.

We'll try to find out more about that comic book in the morning.
I'm sleeping in!
me too.
ahem

Oh shit, Maybe I should have said "hi" to Virgil?

Oh well.

Is it cool if I have this? I found it in the trash.

Dude, you're spilling that shit all over the place. HA HA.

She said it was here someplace

I hate the East side of this town now.
Hey! Who is that?!
Lemme see them lenses, Stoney.
I been watching him since we came over the last knoll. He hasn't moved.
What time did we go to bed last night?

Hmmm, I can't tell who it is,
but he or she ain't moving.
I want to have a look.
You think it's a trap?
I don't see any creep flies.

Weird how he's just sitting there.
I don't think I like it.
Is he holding something?

Woah.

He just fell over.

SHAKEY!
geeze.
Aw, man. Is he dead?
snif snif

uhhhhh
Not quite yet.

C'mon man.
Water.
here.

Why are you out here, Shakey?
GLUG

I've been running and hiding all night trying to get... We were decimated, the Zekes and my sister's gang...
dead,
all
dead.

taken by the creeps.
MY SISTER!

Get OFF me!
All right, man.

Help me get her downstairs.

You mean Olweyez's hole?
Yeah.
Yeah? We're out here looking for it too.

s'over here.
Scientist will fix her, and fix ...

flip
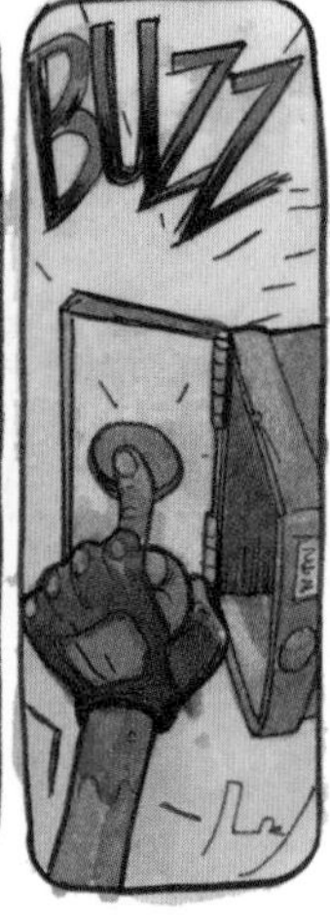
BUZZ

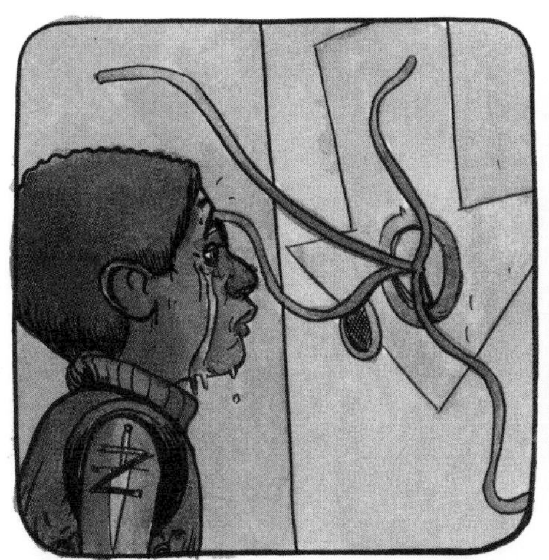

C'mon Olweyez, it's me, Shakey.

zzzip

phip

Pssssssshshsh

Oh! hello! Wow! the Wrenchies! come on.

- Olweyez!

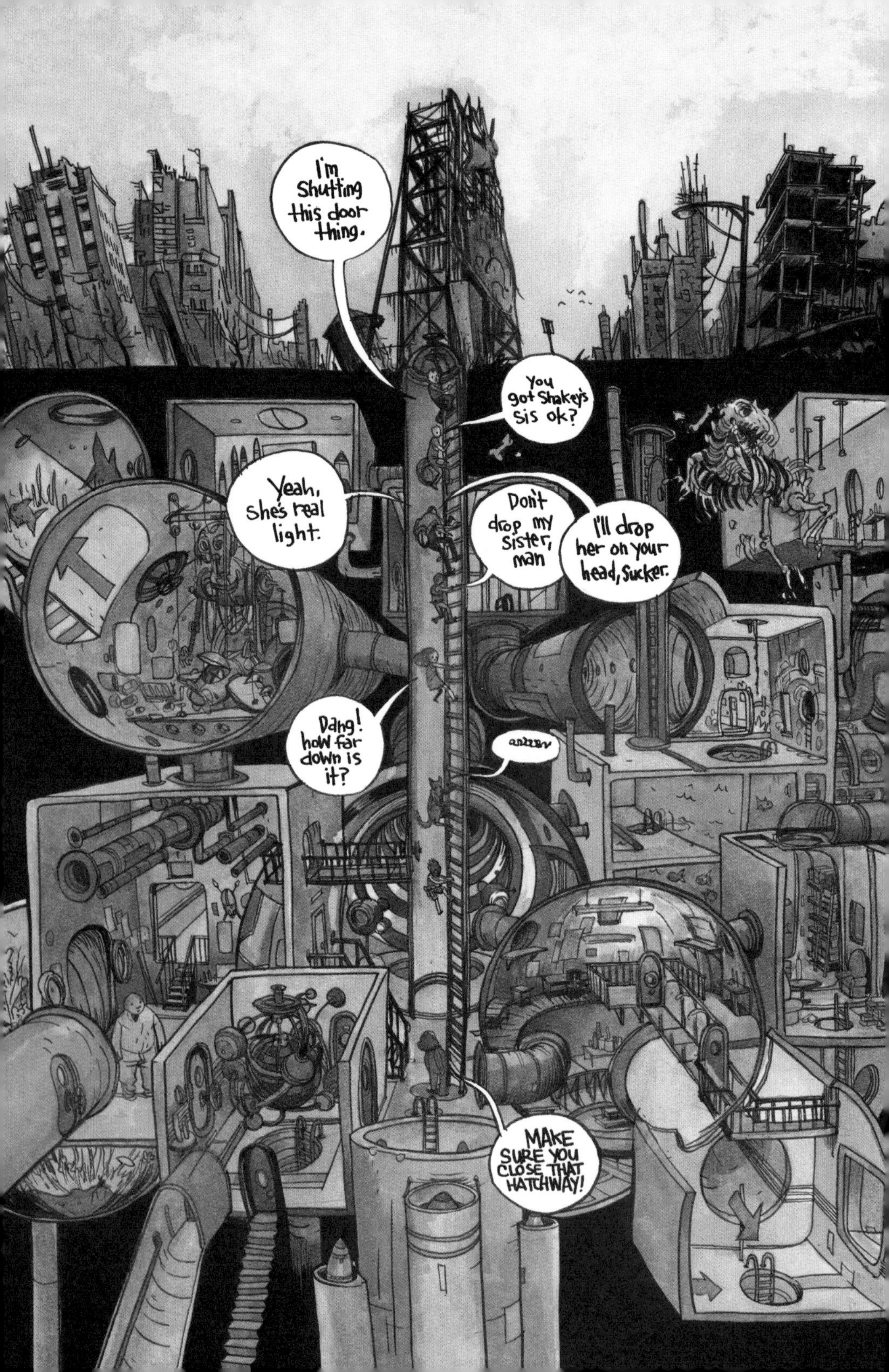
I'm Shutting this door thing.
You got Shakey's sis ok?
Yeah, She's real light.
Don't drop my sister, man
I'll drop her on your head, Sucker.
Dang! how far down is it?
MAKE SURE YOU CLOSE THAT HATCHWAY!

Geeze, Shakey, you guys should get to the infirmary.
hang in there, Sabina.
That is the idea, genius.

heh heh
snort
He knows his way around here.
He's a distant relative of the scientist.
Did you all come to see the scientist?

Show it to him, bro.
It's the Wrenchies issue number one.
I like your house.
snif
This place smells weird.
oh.
put put
Scientist? who's that?

Mmm hmm. I've seen this before. I even decrypted it one night just for kicks.
heh heh.
snif snif
snif snif

SNORT. Let's away to our old library, my young Wrenchies.

The spell is supposed to bring to life the super beings from this book and break the shadowsmen's power by doing so.

Yep, It's all here. All of my notes. :snort: I figured it all out quick, but this was a good puzzle. A lot of work went into it for sure.

FLIP

Besides that comic sort of sucks. huff except for the huff secret code part of huff course.

These are the things that are keeping my spirit renewed these days.

Well, my way is all about perfecting my personal system.

I use my intelligence to see how I can perfect a craft. My belief in myself as an artistic genius tempered with a calculating mind all help me a heck of a lot.

Craft for me is a byproduct of working constantly in a specific manner. In most cases I think that helps me express my ideas effectively.

uhhh

Can you do a drawing of me as one the super-wrenchies guys from that comic?

Here you go, kiddo.
WOW!
Hey, I want one.

So I got to tell you, the chap who created this radical fort is seriously ancient. He built all of this himself a loooong time ago. He is the smartest person in this whole screwed up world.
scratch pick

Despite my own personal distaste for magic and religion he is very holy and exults in all that biz. He'll have a lot more to tell you about that wrenchies comic book.

Soooo, Let us all go and meet the SCIENTIST!

chapter 3
hollis and the ghost

flick
THE GREATEST ERA AT LAST
MAN WILL BE IN CONTROL OF HIS OWN DESTINY THANKS TO THE WRENCHIES
The end
WOW.

Okay, That was a weird comic.
The Wrenchies

I wonder if there are any other issues?
HOLLIS!
PORSCHE

Yeah, Ma! I'm reading.
The Wrenchies

Hollis's apartment. He shares with his mother.
Grown up Sherwood's Place

I met a real live ghost this week.
I think he lives in my neighbor's house.
He's really cool even though he doesn't talk
or do anything except float around a lot.
But he is my friend. We stay up late
and watch tv. We saw some really funny
comedy guys last night on channel 27.
I don't remember who they were but they
were so funny. My favorite stand-up comedians are
Steve Martin and Rich Little. I can do a good Mae West
impersonation but I like being a superhero the best.

What's it supposed to be, a comics book?
It looks sort of gay, I got to say, man.
My cousin has a bunch of these in our basement.
Aw, I could draw better than that, man.
C'mon, you are all free!
C'mon you guys, This is so Coooool.
And it is a COMIC book!
That art does suck, but I like the gun.
Yeah, right! You can't draw, you lying sack of crap.

Danny Sherkat.
the leader
Kelsy Tucker, the ninja
Burton Provance, the brains
the strong guy, Pembroke
Mike Bee Huggins, the humor
Tobin Harrison Pickering, the heart
Comic book? come on, guy.
♫
Must be Hollis.
I was just kidding, Hollis. I like that comic.
snif.
It smells like farts around here.
farts.
...

Check this out.

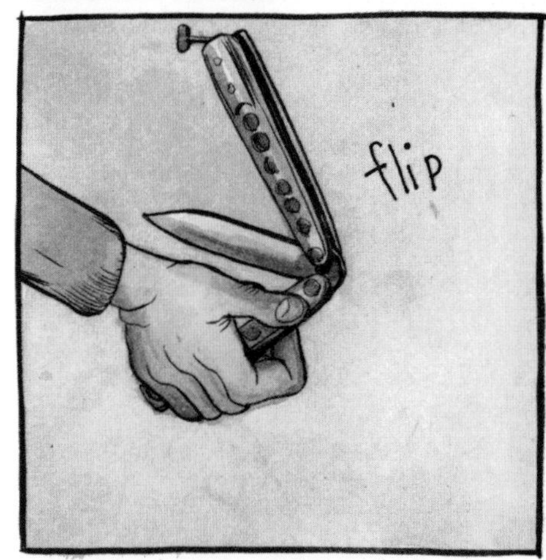
flip

ha–

Don't cut yourself, guy
SWEET! A balisong.
No, dude! THAT is a butterfly knife not a blahblahsong.
yeah.
yeah, man.
yeah.

same thing, Sherlock fuck!
ha.

It's a butterfly knife, douchies.
Snort.
dang.

NO!

Give it here, guy!
Of course, good sir.
cool, I didn't even flinch.

Scratch scratch
scuffle

Hey, Burton, I'm taller than you.
Naw, man.

Yeah, see? 'cause I can see over your head.
Aw, come on, what?

That never works, guy.
Burton is way taller, dorkus.

Nah, man.
Hollis is the dorkus. That's his little stooper-hero suit.

ha ha ha ha ha ha ha

Hey fellows, Know what I got sitting over at my dad's right now? Sumomegasupreme!
Kicking A! you got that new 5,000xz system, right?
so cool, guy.
Burt gets all the best stuff, man. I wish my parents were divorced.
your parents are still married? Gay.
oh. hello.

are you a ghost from Satan?

hmm... if you are,

You are a ghost?

don't come around here any more! ok.

Maybe you can show me the bad movies on the ...dirty channels?

No, I feel bad about asking for that...
I believe you are good.

I'm sorry.

I don't want to be possessed.

I Really like Comics, but all those guys care about are video games and smoking stupid effin' cigarettes.

I'm scared that if I ever have a girlfriend she won't give a crud about my favorite thing in the world. Or if she does like comics she's probably some kind of Jerk.

There are three comic shops in town, but they are all really far from our house. I beg mom all the time to take me there in our car.

She has to drive but when I have a "bad attitude" she won't do it.

It's not fair using comics as blackmail. Maybe comics make me do bad things?

Maybe this wrenchies comic is bad for my soul. What if there is a darkness in my inner spirit man.
It did make me see a ghost.

I know some comic books are way too violent or scary for people to read. But they are not all bad, are they? Just like movies and TV shows. Am I bad for liking stuff? I am sad 'cause there's no one to share my dreams and adventures with.

I hope that one day when I am at school at recess or in church I see that other kid and he's reading a comic or sitting there drawing or maybe pretending he's riding a Taun Taun. I will talk to him and we'll be pals who both like comics and stuff.

This is going to happen soon, I bet.

sigh~

We can hang out until then, though, right?

We will be best pals for many years.
N SYCAMORE
PARKING

Once I become a grown up though I might outgrow the friendship.
PORSCHE
MASTER

We'll both move on to different stuff but we will never ever forget this special time.

Uh-oh ghost, who is that?

GASP

huff huff huff

Mom, there was a bully.

Oh Yeah, She's not home from work yet.

huff huff huff
Now, What's on TV?

4 SALE

My ghost friend!

He lives there?
Or maybe he's just friends with that guy?

That place looks pretty cool.

ahhhhhhhhhhhhhh!

HOLLIS! you're not peeing, are you? You just got into bed!
I'm sorry.
I did it.

I just don't know, ghost... What if this comic book is making me bad?

I want to be a good guy.
rrrip

Maybe I should burn it in case there are demons in it?

Ghost?
Are you mad at me?

FAMILY WOR HIP CENTE
ARATE
THE TRUMPET IN ZION ZION SOUND THE

N THY HOLY MOUNTAIN
I like this song.
BLOW THE TRUMPET IN ZIO

?

OKAY YOUNG MAN, YOU WERE TOLD, "NO TALKING!"
b..b..but I wasn't.

YOU ARE GOING IN THE DIAPER CHAIR!

BABY! BABY! BABY! DIAPER! DIAPER! DIAPER!
Noooooo! I'm not I'm not!

WAYNES
BARBER SH
872
I don't want to go to the Children's church anymore, Mom.
I'm just gonna go to the grown-up service from now on, Okay?

Hey ghost, have you seen my Luke figure anywhere? I lost him I think.

It would be so cool if all this stuff were really real, huh?

Hollis has a dream...
ZZZZZ
Hey guys, does everyone get to have laser guns?

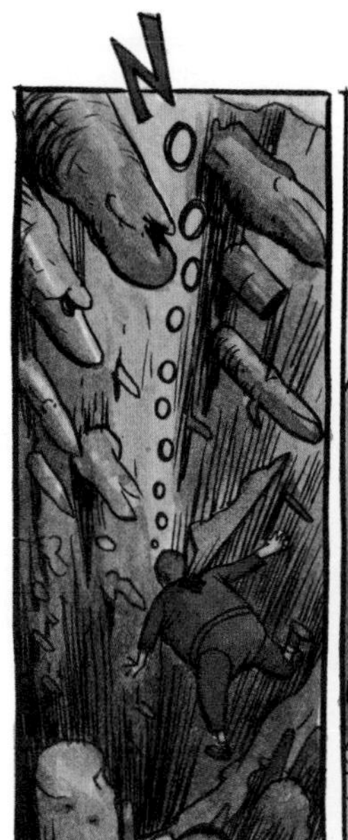
NOOOOOOOOOOOO

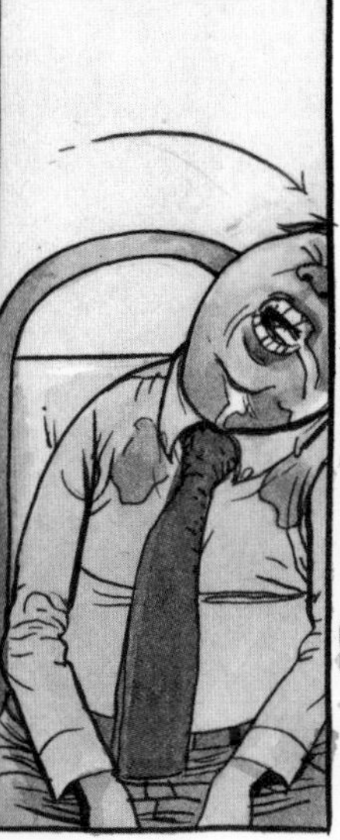

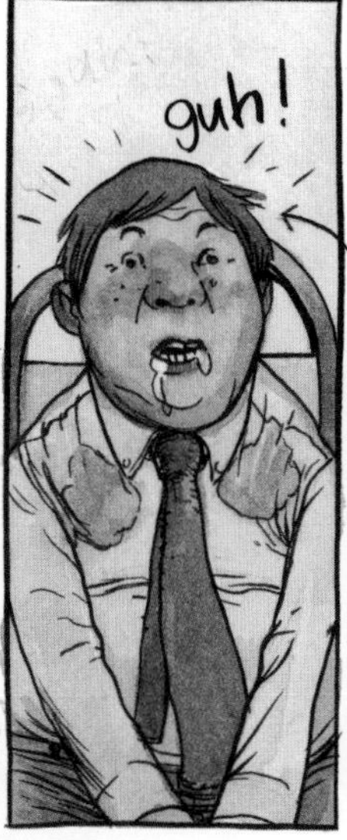
guh!

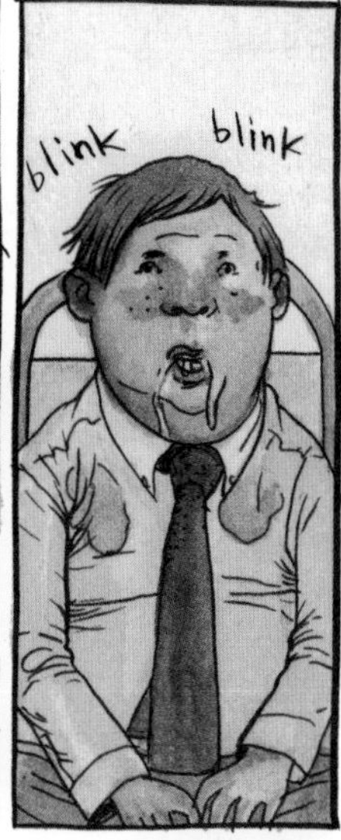
blink
blink

AND HE OPENED THE BOTTOMLESS PIT; AND THERE AROSE A SMOKE OUT OF THE PIT, AS THE SMOKE OF A GREAT FURNACE; AND THE SUN AND THE AIR WERE DARKENED BY REASON OF THE SMOKE OF THE PIT.
AND THERE CAME OUT OF THE SMOKE LOCUSTS UPON THE EARTH: AND UNTO THEM WAS GIVEN POWER, AS THE SCORPIONS OF THE EARTH HAVE POWER AND IT WAS COMMANDED THEM THAT THEY SHOULD NOT HURT THE GRASS OF THE EARTH, NEITHER ANY GREEN THING, NEITHER ANY TREE; BUT ONLY THOSE MEN WHICH HAVE NOT THE SEAL OF GOD IN THEIR FOREHEADS.
amen.
That sounds so cool.
And it's all supposed to happen for real?
WoW.
AND TO THEM IT WAS GIVEN THAT THEY SHOULD NOT KILL THEM, BUT THAT THEY SHOULD BE TORMENTED FIVE MONTHS: AND THEIR TORMENT WAS AS THE TORMENT OF A SCORPION, WHEN HE STRIKETH A MAN. AND IN THOSE DAYS SHALL MEN SEEK DEATH, AND SHALL NOT FIND IT; AND SHALL DESIRE TO DIE, AND DEATH SHALL FLEE FROM THEM.

HEY KID!

OH, HI! you live across from me.
My name is Hollis.
Have you seen the ghost?

?
Uhhh, no...

But I did find this guy hanging out.
I figured he belonged to you.
My Luke!

My name is Sherwood.

NICE CATCH, HOLLIS!

Yeah, I'm good at catching stuff.

MEN
Knock Knock
EW, guy!
Are those your "panties" on the floor?
Oh no! Why did I leave those in there?
What just happened?
What did I just do?

I'm never gonna wear under wear again.

HOLLIS, KEEP YOUR SHOES TIED! OR I'LL JUST GET YOU A PAIR OF LOAFERS!

Noooo MOM! I hate those kind of shoes!

Save 20%
owie. owie. I squatted too long.

OH! Here it is again.
I was stupid for ripping mine up.
the Wrenchies

C'mon, mom. Pleeeease?
the Wrenchies

Why do all these guys look so angry?
Put this back, please. I told you already, we don't have the money for it.

Why are yo
walking sc
funny?
Mo-om! I'm not.

I'm not.

I stole.

I'm a bad guy.

Maybe the ghost made me do it?

No, I'm sorry, God.
Sorry for ALL the bad stuff.
Please Jesus, come into my heart
I want to be good.

Where are you, ghost?
You're my best friend.

Oh.

BULLIES!

Hey!

Why are you bugging these kids? they are under my protection.

snort!-hlhloooo ck

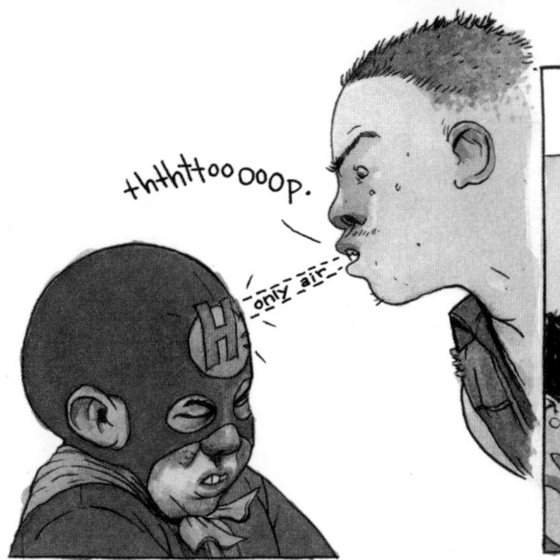
ththttoooooop.
only air

HA HA HAHA HA HA HAHA
Ewwww
Hey where's the spit?

HA HA HAHAHAHAHAHA HA HA
HA HA
Oh, that's an old trick.

AHAH HAH HA!

SPLAT!

gosh.

Hey birdie, did you think it was a real tree? Or maybe it was just your time to pass.
We are so sorry that you had to die.
So we made up this song for you.
ahem
O, bird of wonder, we ask God to let you into heaven.
PARI

Thank you for your sacrifice.
CROW friend
You truly were our friend. amen.

You sure are different, Hollis.

Thanks!

Hey God, how ya doing, friend?

I miss my ghost friend...

and I am sad that the poor bird died,

but I did have a pretty freaking good day today.

yeah.

Grown ups are so weird.

Nasty! That other guy drank too many beers.
Huuooorrk!

They are doing lots of bad stuff over there.

I'm gonna stay up all night. I want to see my ghost friend.
uhhh

ZZZZzz

Snork
Wha?
BANG

Oh my God. It's real magic.
CREAK
I can grasp it.

oooF
uhg
oh.

Ghost, you're back!
Did you just see that?

It looks like that thing on the back of the wrenchies comic book.
I need to go look at that right now.

That Sherwood guy is probably okay, eh ghost?
His apartment stopped glowing, at least.

I'll give it back to him if he asks for it.

It's warm... so pure... and glowy as heck.

Radical! I'm getting into it.

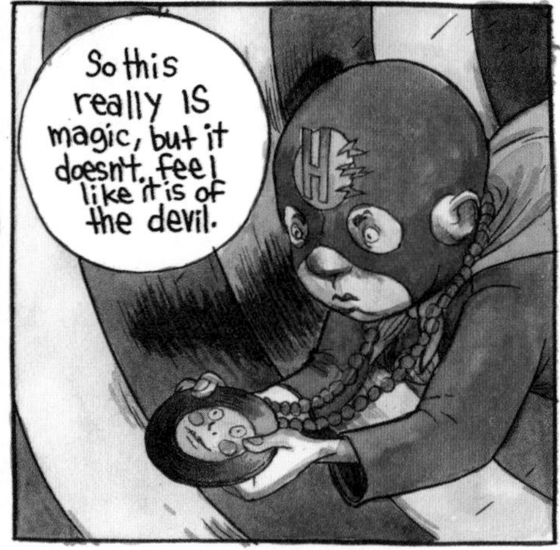
So this really IS magic, but it doesn't feel like it is of the devil.

Don't worry, Hollis.
Okay.

You ARE GOING TO DO FINE.
I want to be a good guy.

I asked Lisa Patterson on the last day of school to "go with me."
Then I didn't call her all summer.
heh
You are such a Jerk, man.
Yeah, guy.

I'm gonna miss you, Mom.
I LOVE YOU, HONEY.
BE CAREFUL.
I'LL PRAY FOR YOU, SON.
I AM PROUD OF YOU.

Ghost.
You're not coming with me?

AND THE FIFTH ANGEL SOUNDED, AND I SAW A STAR FALL FROM HEAVEN UNTO THE EARTH: AND TO HIM WAS GIVEN THE KEY OF THE BOTTOMLESS PIT.
?

Hey, guys.

the Scientist

and original Wrenchies

WELCOME TO MY HOME, THE SOPWITH CAMEL. I AM THE SCIENTIST AND INVENTOR, HERZOG DUKE.
AND YOU, HOLLIS, HAVE JUST EMERGED FROM MY OWN CLEVER INVENTION, THE BRYSON VORTEX TUNNEL.
THE TUNNEL HAS ENABLED US TO TRANSLATE YOU THROUGH A GREAT SPAN OF TIME AND SPACE.

I APOLOGIZE FOR THE ABDUCTION. PLEASE DON'T BE AFRAID. WE WILL NOT HURT YOU. WE ARE YOUR FRIENDS. THANK YOU FOR COMING TO US IN THIS TIME OF SORROW.
AND THANK YOU FOR BRINGING THIS AMULET TO US. AS HAPPY AS WE ALL ARE TO MEET YOU, OUR REAL OBJECTIVE WAS TO ACQUIRE THIS THING. IT HAS BEEN LOST... FOR A LONG TIME.
Don't worry, man, we're cool.
oh.
I'm not in a comic book?
It's just your future.
What can you do?
Snif Snif
I SENT A PROBE THROUGH THE VORTEX TO RETRIEVE THE AMULET, BUT IT HAD TO HAVE YOU, HOLLIS, TO FIND IT'S WAY TO US.
NOW ALL THE ELEMENTS ARE IN PLACE:
• THE DECIPHERED SPELL-CODE IN THE WRENCHIES COMIC BOOK,
• THE COSMIC POWER OF THE MAGIC AMULET,
• THE BRYSON VORTEX TUNNEL AND MY SUPER-COMPUTER,
• ESPIRITO.
SO WITH THE ASSISTANCE OF MY PRODIGIOUS PROTEGÉ, OLWEYEZ,
Hey Sucka'
WE CAN ALL PERFORM A VERY SPECIAL MAGIC RITUAL
ha.
Special magic?
This place is Soooooo cool.
I saw you guys in my dream.
It was a dream.

All right. NOW WE SHOULD ALL GET READY. THE TIMING AND ALIGNMENT MUST BE PRECISE, CHILDREN.
QUICK, CHILDREN, WE MUST HURRY.
Children? Really old Scientist?
Are those your numb-chucks?
I think It's "nun."
OK, So FORM A CIRCLE THERE, DIM THE LIGHTS, AND FIRE UP THE FUSION CORE.
OLWEYEZ, PUT THE RECORD ON AND PLAY IT IN REVERSE.
OK! ·geeze·
please.
Are you crying? Weird.
No. Yeah, I miss Mom.
AW.
c'mon, we all need to be tough.
So cool.
Get in the circle.
Visualize your goal.
oh yeah.
oh yeah.
Turn the knobs,
This is all a steaming sack of bullshit by the way.
OLWEYEZ! HIT THE SWITCH!
flick
mmmmmmmmmmmmmmmmmmmmmmmmmmmmmm

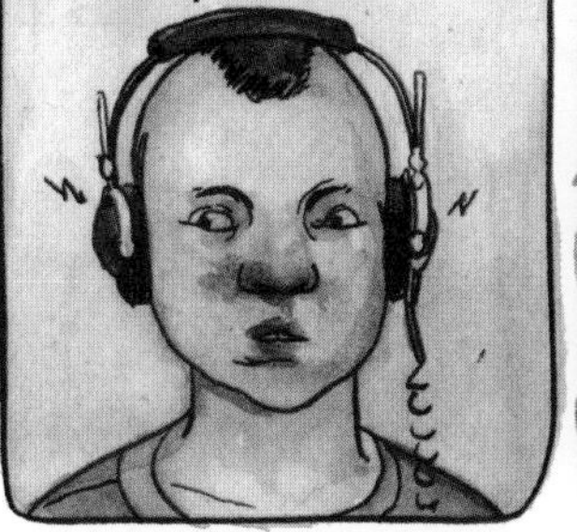

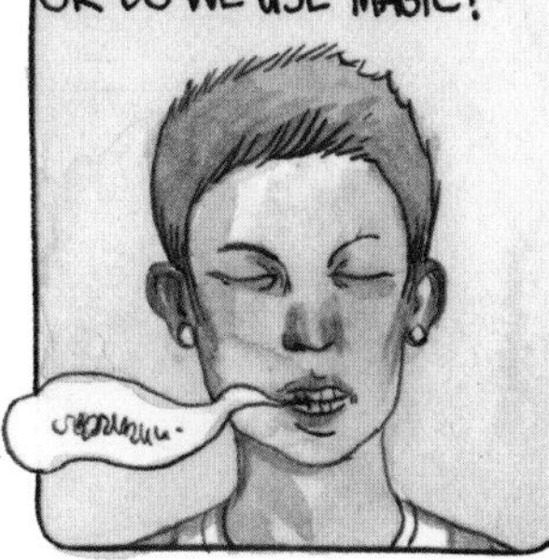

AND LIES,

AND HEARTACHE.

CAN YOU HEAR IT, CHILDREN?

A DISTINCT RESONANCE.

drip

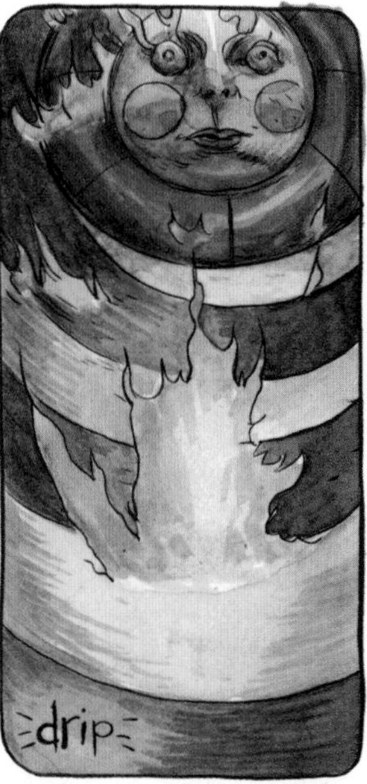

WELCOME ALL OF YOU TO THE HERE AND NOW. WE ARE SO HAPPY TO HAVE YOU.
WELCOME, the Wrenchies.
?
OK
I...
Why...
are my guns bleeding?
Dark-Weird.
What's happening right now?
A lot of little kids are staring at us.
Staring.
S'there something we should be doing, Diamond?
YEAH, AND YOU WANT TO BET IT'S GONNA INVOLVE A LOT OF UGLY VIOLENCE?
vortex bugs
Virgale and Vivian Taylor Supernatural telekinetic psychic twins.
Brian D. O'keefe "the goat" and his sacred blade of eternalness.
Steve "Leking" snipes, Hellfire distributor.
Diamond Day Leadership, Strength, Honor.

VIOLENCE WILL BE REQUIRED.
BUT FIRST...
We like it here.
?
WOW. I AM in a comic.
?
This place can't be real.

REGARDLESS OF WHATEVER YOU CONSIDER "REAL" I ASSURE YOU THERE IS A VERY DEFINITE DANGER IN LETTING ANY OF THESE CREATURES LIVE. WE MUST DESTROY THEM ALL, I'M AFRAID.
IF WE DON'T THEY WILL GROW... GROW INTO SOMETHING... DISEASED, INFECTED BY THE POWER OF SECRET NIGHTMARES.
AS WE ENGAGE IN THIS GRUESOME CHORE I WILL TRY TO OFFER SOME ENCOURAGEMENT AND HELP YOU OVERCOME YOUR OBVIOUS STATE OF CONFUSION.
bzzzt.

EVERY SPELL HAS A COST.

I told you guys he likes to talk.
Sorry bug.
can I have this car?
593-72
AS DETESTABLE THIS IS TO ME THESE BUGS' DEATHS ARE ANOTHER SACRIFICE FOR HUMANITY'S SPIRITUAL REDEMPTION.

YOU SEE, I USED TO HAVE A HUMAN BODY LIKE ALL OF YOU; THIS FORM YOU SEE BEFORE YOU IS NOT THE ONE I WAS BORN TO.

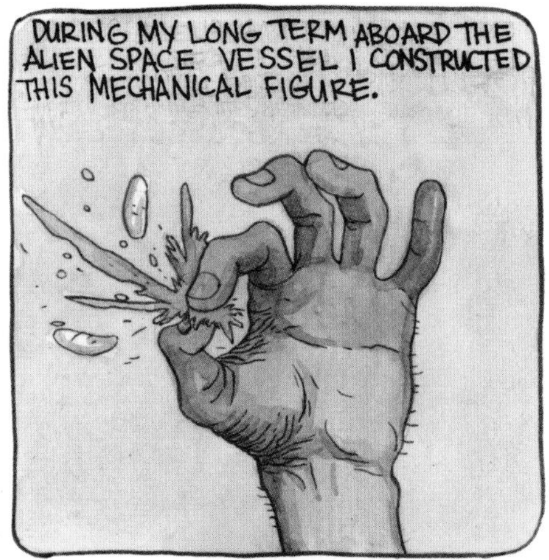
DURING MY LONG TERM ABOARD THE ALIEN SPACE VESSEL I CONSTRUCTED THIS MECHANICAL FIGURE.

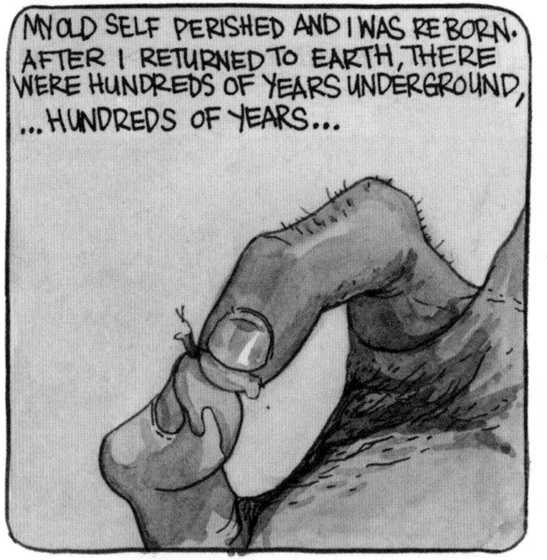
MY OLD SELF PERISHED AND I WAS REBORN. AFTER I RETURNED TO EARTH, THERE WERE HUNDREDS OF YEARS UNDERGROUND, ...HUNDREDS OF YEARS...

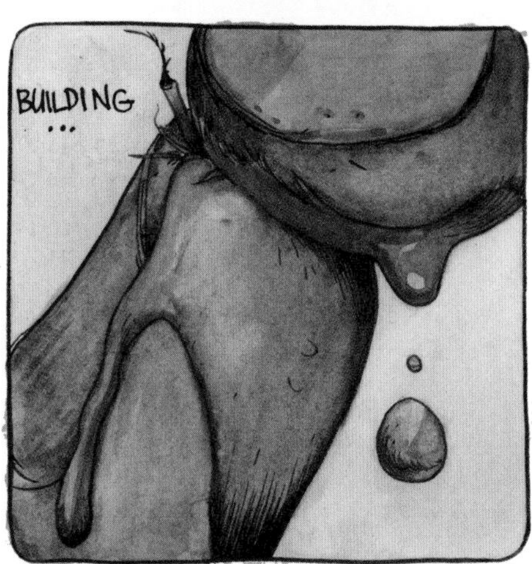
BUILDING ...

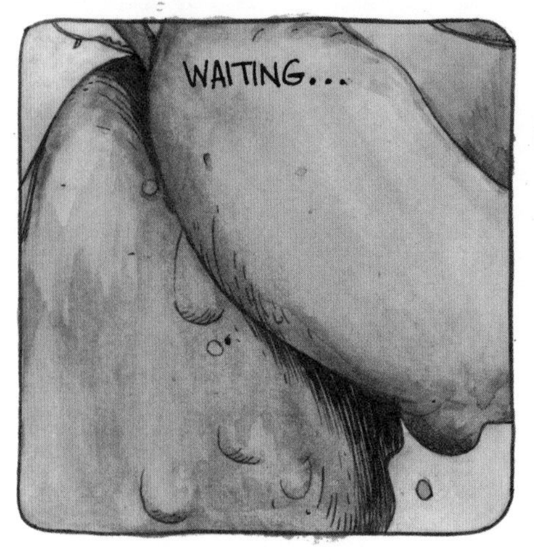
WAITING...

LISTENING TO THE STRANGE EMANATIONS OF THE RADIO.

THE SECRET SIGNALS, THE SOFT CEREBRAL WHISPERS OF A BOY I USED TO KNOW, SHERWOOD PRESLEY BREADCOAT.

I MET YOUNG SHERWOOD DURING OUR MUTUAL IMPRISONMENT ON AN ALIEN SPACECRAFT.
Dr. EXT
Sherwood
Orson
Herzog Duke
Ghost of Ms. Parasol

BEST FRIENDS? YES! WE WERE.
Hey Scientist, What's this guy's name gonna be?
Be delicate and precise, lad!

THEN THE "THING" HAPPENED.

I ESCAPED IN MY NEW BODY, BACK THROUGH THE GALAXY TOWARD EARTH.

SOMEHOW DUE TO TIME/SPACE MECHANICS OF THE ALIEN VESSEL, I HAD ARRIVED AT MY OLD HOME SEVERAL CENTURIES AFTER I HAD LEFT IT.
I DISCOVERED MY ONCE LUSH AND BELOVED EARTH WAS FILTHY WITH DEMONS.

I HID UNDERGROUND. THERE I STARTED MY LONG WORK BUILDING THE SOPWITH CAMEL AND LISTENING TO THE ONLY FORM OF BROADCAST AVAILABLE.

I SPENT DECADES DECIPHERING THE ODD MELODIC MESSAGES, AND EVENTUALLY FOUND THEY ORIGINATED FROM MY OLD FRIEND, SHERWOOD BREADCOAT.
HE INFORMED ME OF MANY SECRETS REGARDING THIS TERRIBLE NEW WORLD.

MUCH OF THE SCIENTIFIC KNOWLEDGE I POSSESSED WAS NOW USELESS. THIS WORLD WAS RULED BY STRANGE MAGIC FROM BEYOND THIS REALM, MAKING TECHNOLOGY UNRELIABLE AND ERRATIC. I MADE MANY FAILED ATTEMPTS AT BUILDING WEAPONS AND ROBOTS TO FIGHT THE SHADOWSMEN. MY EFFORTS WERE EITHER CORRUPTED FOR THEIR USE OR JUST ADDED TO THE WASTE AND POLLUTION. SO I COMMITTED MYSELF TO LEARNING THIS NEW MAGIC AND HELPING THE ONLY HUMANS LEFT, THE CHILDREN.
the Spirit Of the Lord.

DO YOU OBSERVE THE MIRACULOUS FIGHTING PROWESS OF THESE CHILDREN?

HARSH ENVIRONMENT, NEW MYSTIC ENERGY, AND MY OWN SUBTLE HAND HAVE HELPED GIVE THESE YOUNG ONES SOME ACTIVE RESISTANCE TO THE NIGHTMARES.
They fight demons?

you've got to pop off their heads to kill Shadowsmen.
Ha! You do that, kid?

yeah.
urk

TO SURVIVE ON THIS WORLD YOU MUST BE FAST AND STRONG, YOU MUST BE A WARRIOR, YOU MUST LEARN TO FIGHT.
Wait, did he say we were underground?
Yeah, ok.

AND TRY TO KEEP YOUR THOUGHTS POSITIVE. I HAVE BEEN HELPING THE CHILDREN FIGHT DESPAIR SINCE THEIR CONCEPTION.
THIS IS ALL SO CONFUSING.

BORN IN ORBITING LABS,
NURTURED BY THE SUPERNATURAL NEPHALIM.
SHADOWSMEN COME,

DEPOSITED IN RUINS OF THE ANCIENT CITIES, WHICH ARE JUST VAST PRISONS... WAITING AREAS.

REPRODUCING BY INFECTING THE CHILDREN AT THE DAWN OF MATURITY.
RARELY DOES ANY CHILD ESCAPE BEING COMPLETELY CONSUMED.
THEY GET IN THROUGH THE EYES.
actual size of the supernatural nephalim
1ft.
NOT WITH THESE CHILDREN THOUGH. THEY ARE EXCEPTIONAL.
heh.
mm-hm.
...
c'mon.

THEY ARE THE GREATEST FIGHTERS IN THE WORLD. BRUTAL AND WISE, THEY ARE THE FIRST GANG TO HAVE NO FEAR OF THE SHADOWSMEN.

UNRELENTING IN THEIR RESISTANCE TO THE DARKNESS; NOBLE AND JUST, DEDICATED NOT ONLY TO KEEPING EACH OTHER SAFE, THEY ARE COMPASSIONATE AND GENEROUS TO THE WEAK AND OPPRESSED.
ALTHOUGH THESE WRENCHIES HAD NO KNOWLEDGE OF IT, I HAVE BEEN HELPING THEM ALL ALONG AND IN MANY WAYS.
YOU SEE, THE RADIO TOLD ME TO HELP THEM.
THE RADIO TOLD ME TO DO ALL OF IT...

THE NOISES FROM ILLEGAL RADIOS THAT FASCINATE ALL THE CHILDREN ARE TRANSMISSIONS FROM A BOY I ONCE KNEW.
A BOY NAMED SHERWOOD BREADCOAT.

SHERWOOD AND HIS BROTHER ORSON ONCE ENTERED A MAGIC CAVE AND KILLED THE FIRST OF MANY DARK ELVES.

THEY SLEW THOUSANDS OF THOSE WRETCHED CREATURES.

SHERWOOD AND I MET YEARS LATER.
Sheesh, Scientist! this sure is a whole bunch of work.
Totally posatronic.

INEXPLICABLY SHERWOOD RETURNED TO EARTH ONLY MONTHS AFTER HE LEFT, BUT HUNDREDS OF YEARS BEFORE I WOULD MAKE IT BACK.

OVER THE NEXT COUPLE DECADES HE TROD SOME DIFFERENT PATHS:
JUNIOR SPY//ADVENTURER,
If I drop this vial we're all dead.

ART SCHOOL STUDENT,
uhhhhhhhhh
we called the cave, "The Crazy Station."

AND SECRET AGENT.
Shhhhh. secret.

EVENTUALLY HIS GOVERNMENT JOB LEADS TO FRUSTRATION, BOREDOM AND DISILLUSIONMENT.

Just be cool. Be cool. It's ok. Be cool. Be cool. Be cool. Be cool.

HE HAS RECURRING NIGHTMARES HE IS THE ANTI-CHRIST. HE HAS VISIONS OF DESTROYING THE EARTH.

SO HE QUITS HIS JOB AND DEDICATES HIMSELF TO LEARNING WIZARDRY AND MAKING HIS COMIC BOOK.
What's with all the comic book stuff?

HE MIXED HIS OWN BLOOD INTO THE INK HE DREW THE WRENCHIES COMIC WITH.

Wait! I thought that was made by Ms. Parasol?
SIMPLY A NOM DE PLUME, CHILD.

OH, "anomdy ploome," I get it.
Hey! I know that guy Sherwood. He's my neighbor. He made the Wrenchies?! No stinking way!

HE DID, HOLLIS, AND ALSO GAVE YOU THE AMULET.
Yeah, He gave it to me.
I didn't steal it.

HE SAW WITHIN YOU A WARRIOR'S HEART!

YOU ARE SPECIAL, HOLLIS.
YOU LEAPT.
YOU GRASPED IT WITHOUT HESITATION. SHERWOOD KNEW YOU WOULD OR HE WOULDN'T HAVE BESTOWED THIS POWERFUL OBJECT UPON YOU.
What about my mom, though?
?

HE CREATED THE WRENCHIES. HE CREATED YOU.
I know I know that name, "Sherwood Breadcoat." Why does it sound so familiar?
bzt

WE JUST PULLED YOU OUT OF THE AMULET WHERE SHERWOOD HID YOUR SOULS.
Splat.
Huh?
SPLAT

HE DESTROYED WHO YOU ONCE WERE AND RE-CREATED YOU AS SUPER-BEINGS.
Our lives.
Our lives are a lie?

NOT A LIE. YOU JUST LIVED A DIFFERENT LIFE BEFORE YOU ANSWERED SHERWOOD'S CALL.
I...I remember something... like a dream.
splat

THE ADVERTISEMENT YOU READ CONTAINED A HIDDEN SUGGESTION.
splat
Nomdy Ploome!

OF ALL THE MILLIONS OF PEOPLE THAT SAW THOSE ADVERTISEMENTS ONLY FIVE RESPONDED TO ITS CRYPTIC INVITATION.
They give me so much shit?
Just 'cause I'm a wizard?
fuck it!
bzt.
?

THE FIVE OF YOU:
Leking, No regrets, There was nothing left for you there.
Virgale and Vivian, the carousel ride was cruel and grotesque.
Diamond, All talent and no passion.
Goat the truth nearly broke you.

But I don't remember any of that.
No, YOU ONLY KNOW A LIFE IN WHICH YOU WERE A GREAT HERO... FIRST LIVED IN THE PAGES OF A COMIC BOOK, THEN INSIDE THE AMULET, IN A SUB-COSMIC TRAINING WORLD.

YOU ALL SUBMITTED WILLINGLY...

AND WERE CAST INTO AN INTERIOR CRYSTAL DIMENSION OF THE AMULET, WHERE YOU LIVED AS HEROIC WARRIORS FOR WHAT SEEMED TO YOU SEVERAL YEARS.

IT WAS THE ONLY WAY SHERWOOD KNEW OF TO MANIFEST YOU BACK IN OUR WORLD.

EVERY SPELL HAS ITS COST.

SHERWOOD'S VISIONS SHOWED HE WOULD BE HUMANITY'S DESTROYER. HE CREATED YOU ALL AS A FAILSAFE.

ONLY HE DIDN'T HAVE TIME TO FINISH THE SPELL AND DRAW YOU OUT BEFORE THE SHADOWS MEN TOOK HIM.
-rats.

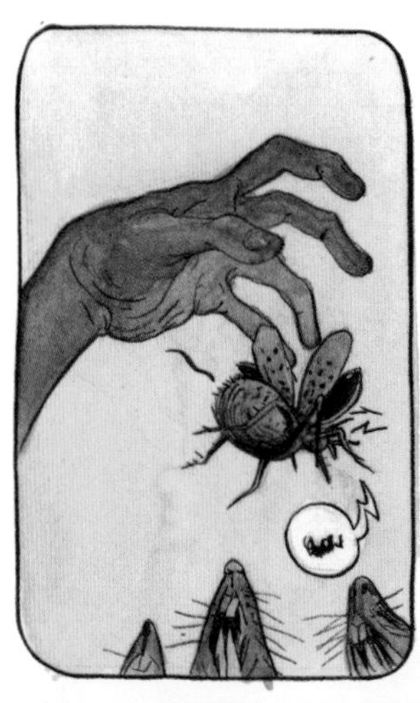

SHADOWSMEN GOT TO SHERWOOD BEFORE HE COULD PULL THE WRENCHIES BACK OUT OF THE AMULET.
So, uh... someone made a comic about us?
C'mon, Goat.

SHERWOOD HAD SENT OUT A DISTRESS CALL TO FIND ANOTHER WIZARD TO DO THE CONJURING.
!

BUT NO WIZARD EVER CAME TO HIM.

SO HE HID THE AMULET RIGHT BEFORE HE WAS TAKEN.
dang!

THE BIGGEST FLAW IN SHERWOOD'S COMPLICATED PLAN WAS WASTING YEARS DRAWING THE COMIC BOOK. A COMIC BOOK? HOW FOOLISH TO USE THAT AS A MEDIUM. NOT MANY PEOPLE READ COMICS.

Yeah, all my pals just play video games.

thup thup
But I'm glad he made it. I like it.

IT JUST TOOK HIM TOO LONG TO DO ALL THAT DRAWING. THEN HALF OF THE PRINT RUN WAS LOST, AND EVEN WITH THE INEXPENSIVE COVER PRICE NO ONE BOUGHT THE BOOK EXCEPT FOR A FEW WEIRD CHILDREN.

Oh! No OFFENSE, HOLLIS.
Um, I stole it.
pick
pick
I'm Sorry.
rub
rub
It's OKAY, HOLLIS.
WE ALL THINK YOU'RE COOL.
SHERWOOD LOST SO MUCH PRECIOUS TIME MAKING THAT BOOK; HE LOST HIS MIND, THEN HE LOST HIS BEST FRIEND...
Sherwood's best pal,
Fortune Sceptre
exit
entry
THEN HE LOST HIS OWN SPIRIT AND THE WORLD HE WAS TRYING TO SAVE.
espirito santo

"I reached for my amulet but it was gone..."

VOLCANOES WORLDWIDE ERUPTED SIMULTANEOUSLY, CHOKING EVERYTHING WITH ASH.

EARTHQUAKES, RAMPANT PESTILENCE AND WARS UPON BLOODY WARS.

ONE RATHER LARGE METEOR STRUCK THE EARTH. SO NATURALLY THE GATE TO HELL WAS TORN OPEN.

THE WORLD HAS EVER SINCE BEEN SUBJECTED TO THE SHADOWSMEN. THEY LINE THE ATMOSPHERE NEARLY SHOULDER TO SHOULDER.

THE SOURCE OF THEIR POWER, THE BODY OF SHERWOOD, A PERFECT CONDUIT FOR EXTRADIMENSIONAL COSMIC ENERGIES.

FROM HIM NEW POWER FLOWED INTO THIS WORLD.

ALL OF THE STORED METAPHYSICAL ENERGY FROM KILLING DEMONS AND YEARS OF EXPOSURE TO THE AMULET'S ENIGMATIC RADIATION PRIMED HIS BODY FOR SUCH A PURPOSE.

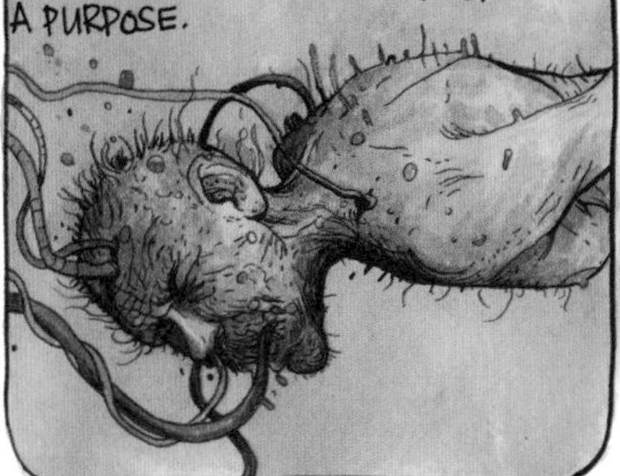

THE SHADOWSMEN'S SINISTER DEVICES HAVE KEPT SHERWOOD BARELY ALIVE AND CONSTANTLY DREAMING. SHERWOOD'S INSANE DREAMS ARE LIKE A MAGIC INFUSED FEAST FOR THE DARK ONES WHO FEED OFF FEAR AND NIGHTMARES.

BUT LONG AGO SHERWOOD HAD FORESEEN THAT WITH YOUR AMAZING ABILITIES, YOU WRENCHIES COULD BREAK THE POWER OF THE SHADOWSMEN AND SAVE SHERWOOD'S BODY FROM DEFILEMENT.

THE CRYPTIC MUSIC ON THE RADIO INFORMED ME OF THE CHILDREN FINDING THE WRENCHIES COMIC. THE ESPIRITO MACHINE CONFIRMED YOU WOULD ALL COME HERE TO ME.

Super computer Espirito Sancto

ESPIRITO SANCTO

wand

I ALSO KNOW THAT WE CAN'T USE THE BRYSON TUNNEL OR ANY OF MY VEHICLES TO DELIVER US TO OUR OBJECTIVE, THE SECRET COMPOUND OF THE DARK ELVES.

THAT PLACE CAN ONLY BE APPROACHED ON FOOT.

THAT IS CRUCIAL IN BREAKING THE GRIP THE SHADOWSMEN HAVE ON THIS WORLD.
We have to kill that Sherwood guy?
But we'll still get to kill monsters, right?
YES, BE ASSURED, YOUNG BANCE WE WILL KILL MANY MONSTERS ON OUR QUEST.
Ok, good.
floating n labs
WALKING A PARTICULAR PATH THROUGH THE WASTES THERE WILL BE CONSIDERABLE CHALLENGES.
OUR ROAD HAS NO VISIBLE TRAIL BUT ESPIRITO HAS MAPPED THE ROUTE.
A LONG AND TERRIBLE PROGRESS, TRACING AN ARCANE PATTERN ON FOOT,
THE WALK WILL BE A PERFORMANCE OF A COMPLEX SPELL THAT WILL GAIN US ADMITTANCE TO THE WRETCHED HIVE.

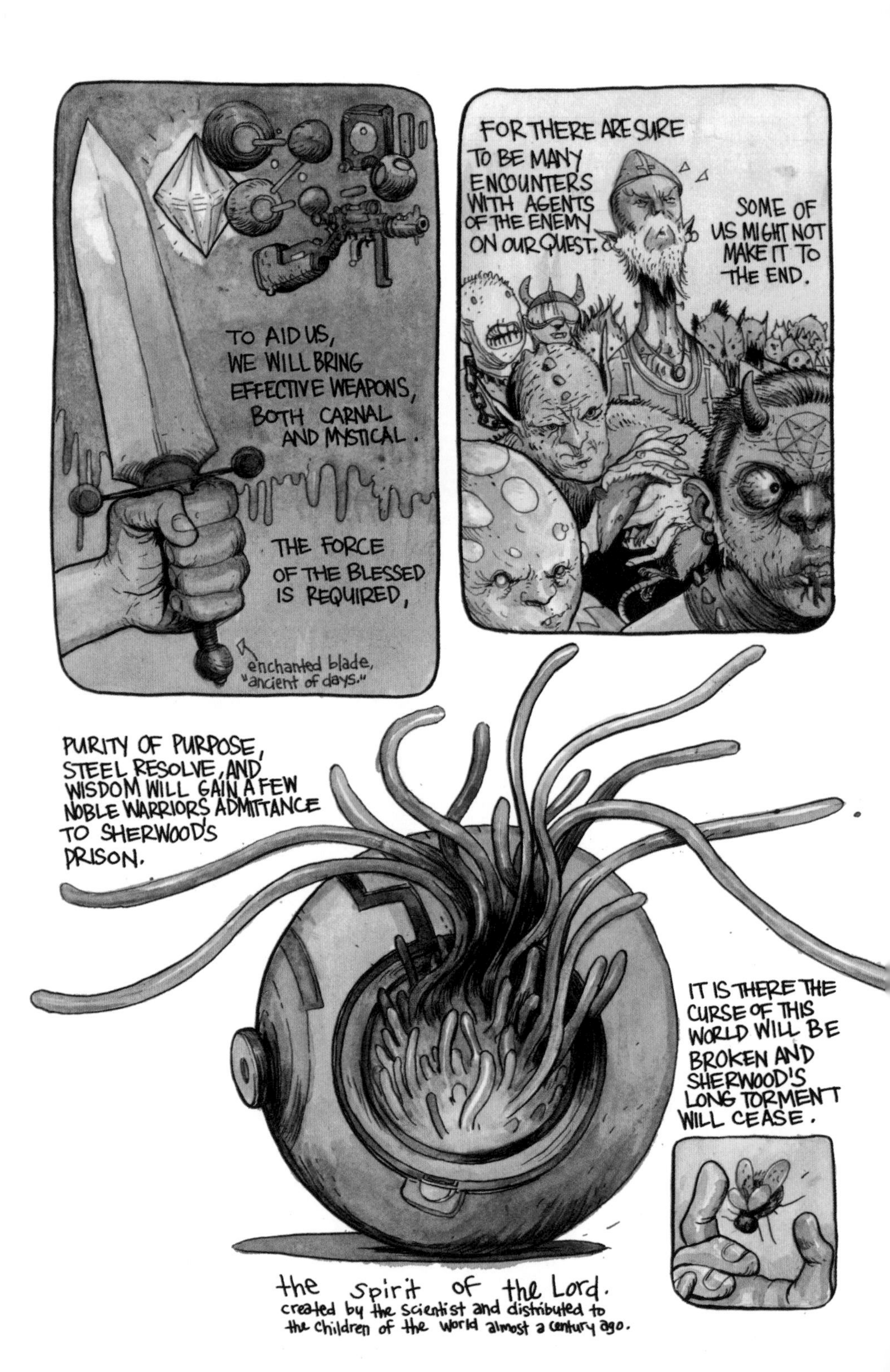
TO AID US,
WE WILL BRING
EFFECTIVE WEAPONS,
BOTH CARNAL
AND MYSTICAL.
THE FORCE
OF THE BLESSED
IS REQUIRED,
enchanted blade,
"ancient of days."
FOR THERE ARE SURE
TO BE MANY
ENCOUNTERS
WITH AGENTS
OF THE ENEMY
ON OUR QUEST.
SOME OF
US MIGHT NOT
MAKE IT TO
THE END.
PURITY OF PURPOSE,
STEEL RESOLVE, AND
WISDOM WILL GAIN A FEW
NOBLE WARRIORS ADMITTANCE
TO SHERWOOD'S
PRISON.
IT IS THERE THE
CURSE OF THIS
WORLD WILL BE
BROKEN AND
SHERWOOD'S
LONG TORMENT
WILL CEASE.
the spirit of the Lord.
created by the scientist and distributed to
the children of the world almost a century ago.

squish
OKAY, THAT WAS THE LAST BUG. NOW, LET ME GIVE YOU A QUICK TOUR OF MY HOME.
I THINK YOU MIGHT LIKE IT.
I am Pretty proud of it, actually.
IF YOU GOT SUCH A NICE BIG PLACE...then... Why not let kids stay here? And...
Do you have a TV?

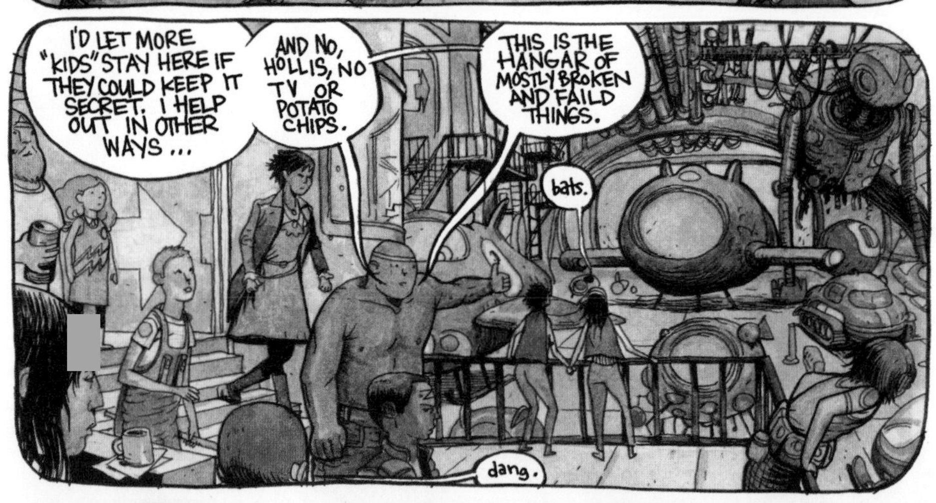
I'D LET MORE "KIDS" STAY HERE IF THEY COULD KEEP IT SECRET. I HELP OUT IN OTHER WAYS ...
AND NO, HOLLIS, NO TV OR POTATO CHIPS.
THIS IS THE HANGAR OF MOSTLY BROKEN AND FAILD THINGS.
bats.
dang.

Say... Where's Olweyez?
Gun guy too?
THIS IS, THE GREAT HALL...
!
great.
What about Coffee?
Do We still have that in the future?
snif

the Stellar chamber
EXIT
the exhausted armory
THESE GARDENS WERE MEANT TO BE AN EDEN WHERE CHILDREN COULD GROW THEIR OWN FOOD.
UNFORTUNATELY MY ATTEMPTS AT HORTICULTURE PROVED DISASTEROUS. THE FRUIT IS INEDIBLE, THE VEGETABLES ARE POISON.
THE YOUNG WRENCHIES AND SOME OTHERS HAVE BEEN QUITE SUCCESSFUL AT CULTIVATING UNDER-GROUND GARDENS AND FINDING ANCIENT CACHES OF SUSTENANCE.
THEY HAVE GREATER RESISTANCE TO THE EVILS OF THIS WORLD BY NEVER HAVING CONSUMED THE SHADOWSMEN'S CORRUPTED JUNK FOOD.
God dang big.
Now how come I've never seen THIS room before?
!
Why can't we just live here?
Our fort is pretty cool too, you know.
!
Wow.
Uh-huh, The creeps, vending machines will mess with your guts.
You got to be kidding my ass.
Yeah, man, when are we gonna go out and kill some demons?

theatre of the upset.
Underground coffee shop.
So... you are calling THIS coffee?
BUT MOST CHILDREN SURVIVE HOWEVER THEY CAN BY FORAGING THROUGH THE AMPLE TRASH ON THE SURFACE, HUNTING INFECTIOUS VERMIN, TAKING FROM THE CREEP'S EVIL VENDING MACHINES, OR EVEN MOST GRUESOMELY, RESORTING TO CANNIBALISM.
I HAVE STRIVED TO PROVIDE PROPER NOURISHMENT TO THE YOUNG ONES WHEN I CAN; PROTEIN PASTES AND VITA-SUPPLEMENTS, BUT CHILDREN STILL STARVE.
MY ATTENTIONS OVER THE YEARS HAD TO BE MORE FOCUSED ON KEEPING MY EXISTENCE AND THE SOPWITH CAMEL A SECRET, LOCATING THE AMULET, AND DRAWING ALL OF YOU WRENCHIES UNTO ME. I AM ONLY CAPABLE OF SO MUCH.

A few corridors away...
So many doors in this hideout.

?
Hey, gun guy.

Time for me to play fishie.

But we should chat some-time.

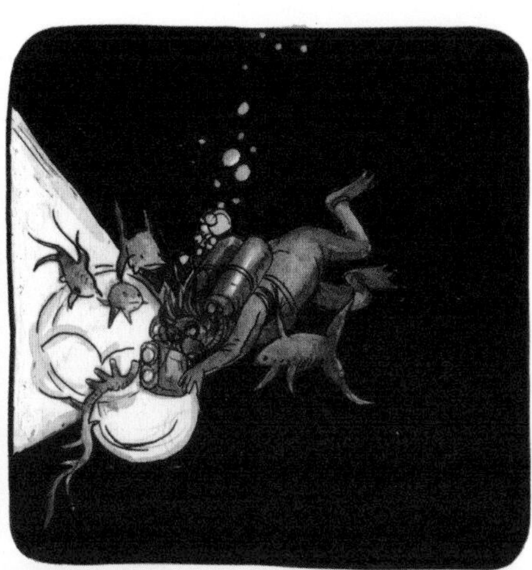

'kay.

Back in the garden...

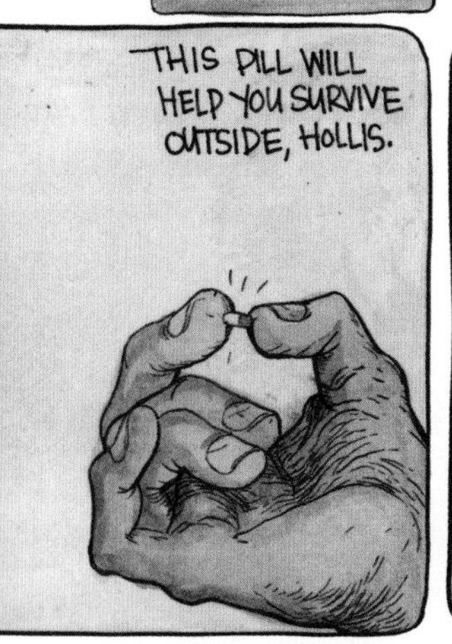

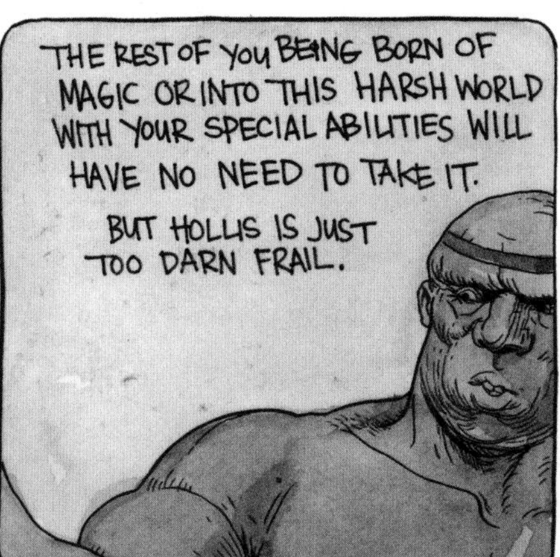

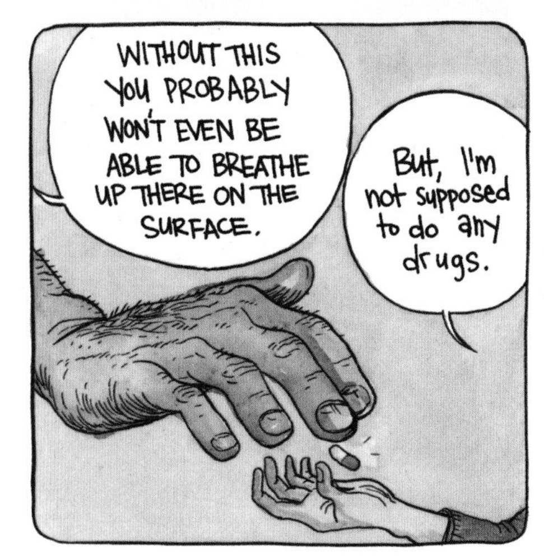

OH UH, SURE, HERE YOU GO. I GUESS IT'S GOOD FOR YOU, LIKE A SUPER VITAMIN OR SOMETHING.

the scientist has the best water.
glurg.
let's save ours for later.
Drugs are dumb.
later on...
in the PLANNING ROOM.
WELL... THAT COVERS THE WHOLE PLAN. IT COULD TAKE US YEARS BUT WITH OUR COMBINED MIGHT I AM CONFIDENT WE CAN OVERTHROW THE SHADOWSMEN.

BUT I SUGGEST WE LEAVE NOW; THE ALIGNMENT MUST BE JUST RIGHT.
Yeah, we can do this. Everyone should go get outfitted and geared up for the road.
Good, I can't absorb any more information; I could absorb some more beers though... about seventeen or so...
Scientist has it all worked out.
ahem
This weird kid, again?
I'm gonna stay.
tap tap..
Someone has to watch the fort and...
It's just too scary for me up there.
I like it here and...
I'm not brave like you guys.

Even later still in Supplies/Wardrobe.
What's up, dog?
THE WRENCHIES HAVE WELCOMED YOU AS ONE OF THEIR OWN, SHAKEY.
Yeah, I know.
YET YOU STILL BEAR THE SIGN OF THE ZEKES, TO HONOR THEIR MEMORY?
WOOF
tug tug
EXIT

Yeah. I miss those guys...
Scientist, I really fucked up bad.
WE ARE ALL HUMAN, SHAKEY.
I'M PROUD OF YOU.

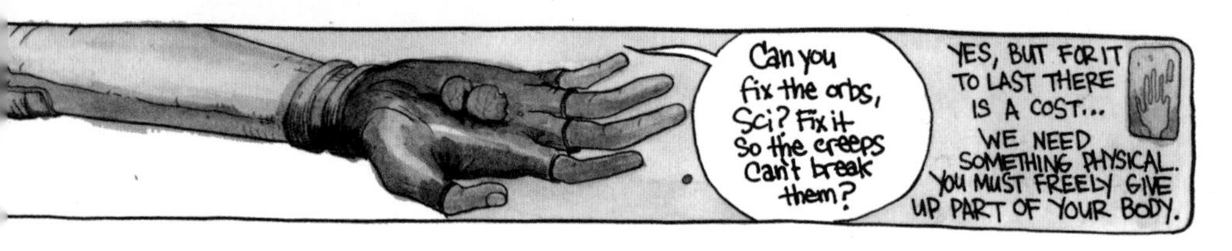
Can you fix the orbs, Sci? Fix it so the creeps can't break them?
YES, BUT FOR IT TO LAST THERE IS A COST... WE NEED SOMETHING PHYSICAL. YOU MUST FREELY GIVE UP PART OF YOUR BODY.

I AM SORRY.
S'ok; It's worth it to me.
THEN PLACE YOUR HAND AND YOUR SPHERES INSIDE THE OCTOBER CHAMBER.
ok.
Every spell has it's cost, eh?
DANGER
I'm glad you're feeling better, sis.
barf.

And so...
I got a bag full of good throwin' rocks.
...
I like my new belt.
!
Looks like we are all hooked up and hauling ass.
Every-thing is right.
SOON WE WILL TRULY BE HAULING ASS. PREPARE FOR OUR ASCENSION TO THE SURFACE!
Still feeling that pill.
bye guys.

chapter 5 the quest

Hey God, Hollis here again. It has been a while since we last chatted, eh?
My dang eyes are really starting to burn and sting from the crummy air. We've been walking for so long, weeks maybe even.
But I really like it. I only feel tired at night really, and there is so much cool stuff to see.
Sometimes it's scary stuff though.
On the very first day we left the underground, we met some old pal of the wrenchies.
fortune?
fortune...

oh no.
Hey.

You okay, man?

I'm Sorry.

Why'd you kill me, pal?

It's all bullshit!

Everything happened so dang fast.
THIS IS BAD MAGIC, BUT I THINK I CAN COVER IT.
My guts felt real gross...
GOAT! feel that?
Yep.
IS this all really happening?
?
AW, these're easy.

But it was cool, the wrenchies all knew how to really fight.

blam!
blam!
?

Ha, and that little kid Tad is always following gun guy around.
twang!

I like those guys.

BOOM!
CINDERDEMONS, THESE PARTICULAR ONES CAN NOT COEXIST WITH MUSIC.
dang.

can we put this one on next?
hell yes, buddy

That got all the rest of the evil ones...

but...

One of the psychic twins got killed.

that was real sad.
her body just melted away.

THE MAGIC RECORDS ARE NOT AS EFFECTIVE ON EVERY SORT OF EVIL.
AS WE ENCOUNTER VARIOUS AGENTS OF THE ENEMY WE NEGOTIATE EACH ONE FREE OF ROUTINE.
SHADOWSMEN FOR INSTANCE, REQUIRE A MORE DIRECT AND GRIM METHOD OF DISPATCH.
yeah,
I like the nights because we all sleep in a force field.

Separating the head from the neck is the only way to kill Shadowsmen.
And be sure to destroy the head too, suckers.
AH, YES,
I STILL MARVEL AT THE MAGICAL AND WONDEROUS POSSIBILITIES OF THIS PLACE,
BUT THERE IS A DEEP CORRUPTION WE CAN SENSE ALL AROUND US.
yeah.
destroy all their fuckin' heads
sob
I like this house.
y-yeah.
It's a bubble, sorta like a snow globe.
I've always really liked those.
WE MUST EXCISE THIS EVIL SO MAN CAN LIVE AGAIN.
yeah, yeah, we get it.

"Great evil; must be excised." that is like the millionth time you've told us, Sire.
Nice chin dribble, and don't exaggerate Goat.
Whoah.
Why're you being a dick?
old people are weird.
Yikes.
Aw, I remember it. The old world wasn't all that great anyway.
gosh, sorry guys.
I don't buy all that "good old days" malarky.
The World's as fucked as it ever was-
lick
ta hell with nostalgia.
BUT CAN'T YOU FEEL THE EVIL?!
I'm gonna shut up for the rest of the night.
Yes.
?
ONCE WE ELIMINATE SHERWOOD AND DISRUPT EVIL'S HOLD ON THIS PLANET YOU WILL SEE-
Ok, I think I can feel it now.
Goat was right.
Wait, I'm not thinking straight.
can't... can't even smoke here.
fuuuhh
Bluurrg
ew

I miss my mom and tv real bad.

I miss my mom the most of course.

I keep hearing her voice say the same thing,

The devil is trying to destroy your life.

God, please tell Mom I'll be good.

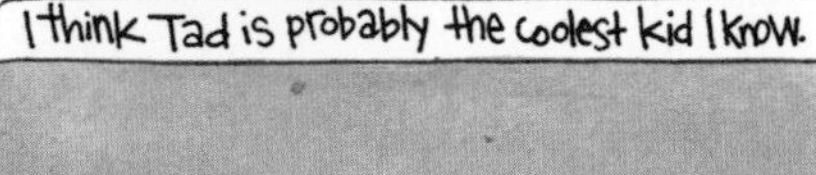

After the bugs left, psi-girl's hair and clothes and everything all turned white.
We think she just walked off by herself. No one ever saw her again.

What the hell, Scientist? All our food and two of my team mates are gone!
And why can't we get a decent cup of coffee going?

I'M SORRY THIS... THIS IS NOT ALL PROCEEDING AS I HAD PREDICTED IT WOULD, I... I DON'T-
Bance and Mars have been teaching me how to throw ninja stars.
Yeah, we are all feeling anxiety, feeling that darkness...
each of us, all so alone.
bullseye!
tok

THE VERY AIR OUT HERE SEEMS TO IMBUE EVERYTHING WITH FAILURE.
Well Maybe we should all spend some time meditating in the mornings?

scientist made this cool thing that holds all of our stuff so the bugs can't get at it again.
Not a bad idea, really.
supplies

And scientist can Just shrink it down and put it in his pocket.

scientist told me to keep the amulet safe. The Shadowsmen don't really care about it, or don4 know how to use it or something like that.
It's invisible to them and is supposed to protect me too.
A little bit ago my ghost pal showed up. I don't know how he got here but I was so happy to see him again.
He hangs out with us now but no one else can see him I think, except maybe for the scientist. He wont look at me when I talk about it...
Oh well, I really like my ghost, pal.

WE ALL REQUIRE OUR OWN WAY OF DEALING.
TOXINS, POLLUTION, RADIATION, MAGIC.
PILLS HELP COUNTER THE CORRUPTION.
THE CHILDREN RELY ON THE PILLS, LE KING.
pills are good.
OH HO, LOOK HERE.
Lemme see.
Why do you kids take so many pills?
What are you, square?

We had a real bad day this week. It started out ok because we found a clothes making machine, but then it got real cruddy when we all were ambushed in this crazy old building.
Aw, these are all over the place.
INDEED, AND EVEN STRANGER, MOST OF THEM STILL FUNCTION.
Whoah, new fur cape, Cap'n? present?
Please ... be aware, Be present.
gulp.
IN THIS BROKEN WORLD THERE IS AT LEAST ONE DECENT AND BENEFICIAL DEVICE LEFT US BY MAN.
LOOKS LIKE POWER IS STILL GOOD.
I'M GOING TO START IT UP, OK?
The worst thing was I saw a bunch of dead bodies, undissolved people piled next to the machine and nobody except me even noticed them.
POWER ON

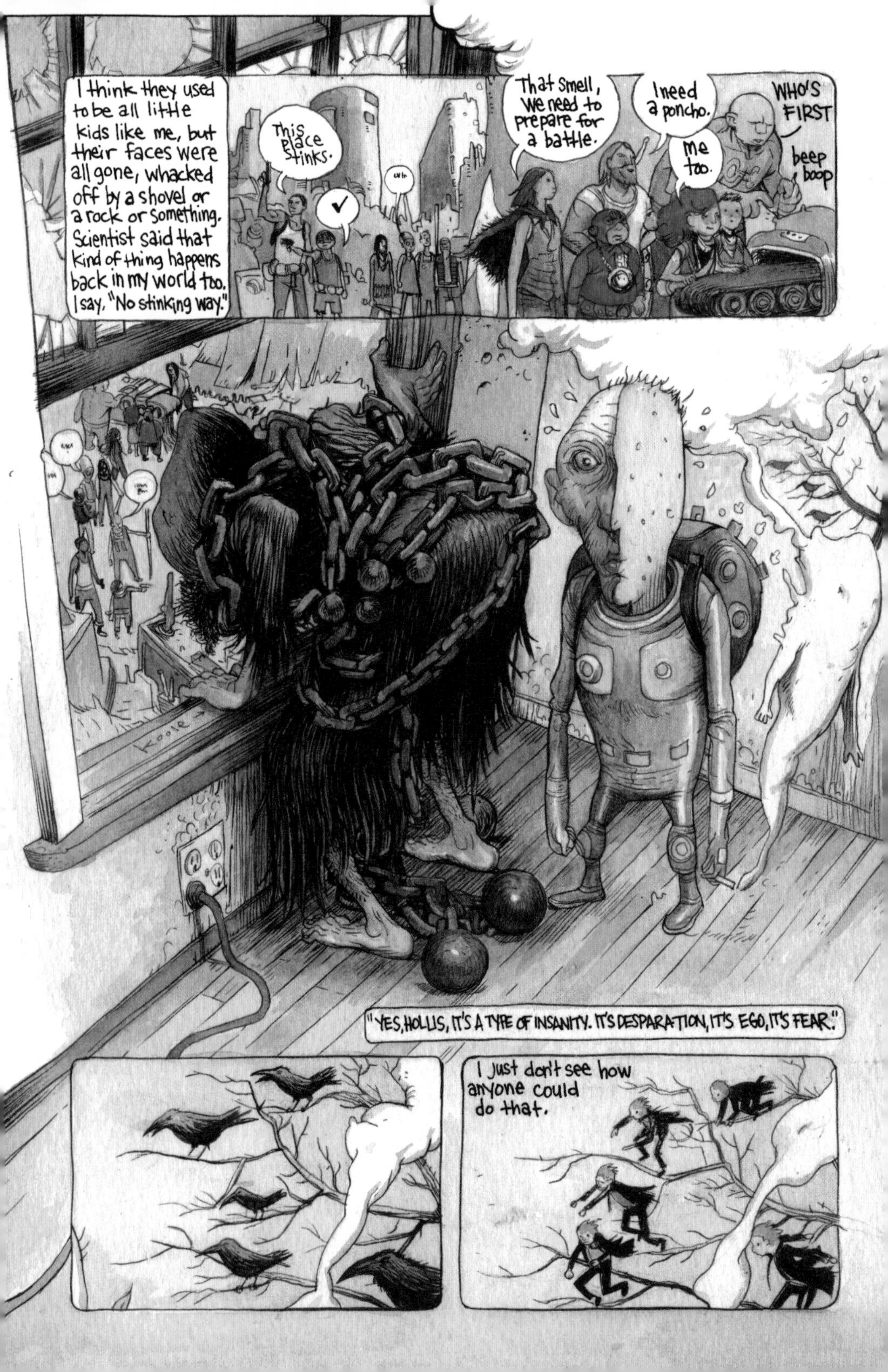

I think they used to be all little kids like me, but their faces were all gone, whacked off by a shovel or a rock or something. Scientist said that kind of thing happens back in my world too. I say, "No stinking way."
This place stinks.
✓
That smell, we need to prepare for a battle.
I need a poncho.
Me too.
WHO'S FIRST
beep boop
KOOLE
"YES, HOLLIS, IT'S A TYPE OF INSANITY. IT'S DESPARATION, IT'S EGO, IT'S FEAR."
I just don't see how anyone could do that.

IT IS PRIDE, THE COMPLETE ANTI-PRESENCE.
Actually The cape WAS indeed a present from the dark beast, who wore it as its genuine hide.
No Shit?
Anti-presents?

WE ARE ALL CAPABLE OF MANY HORRIBLE THINGS.
Its ghost gave it to me in return for a sweet release from the pain of this world.
I like her old suit better.
Good one, Cap'n.
What?!

Fearless, be fucking fearless, man.
ACKNOWLEDGMENT BRINGS AWARENESS.

ALL THINGS MUST CHANGE FORM.

EVERYTHING IS CONSTANTLY TRANSFORMING.

GO my minions, servants of my ill will, you deal with these interlopers!
Go do my bidding.
NOW.
Screw off, you manacled, derelict, Rasputin.
I control you.
Yeah, yeah.

LEARN TO ACCEPT WHAT IS, HOLLIS.
The scientist sure messes up a lot. The grown-ups all act like they know what they are doing, but I think they are really just faking it.
I think the smoke is really just a metaphor or something.
Stab you.
sklork
The smoke got in all our heads too.
Fuck this smoke.
Yesss, control you.
Sorry, Kids.
bang bang
Control shit and die, Jacob Marley monk mother fucker.
kpow

I have trouble remembering it right, everything being smoky and upside-downy.

Bance was the only one that could see through it somehow...

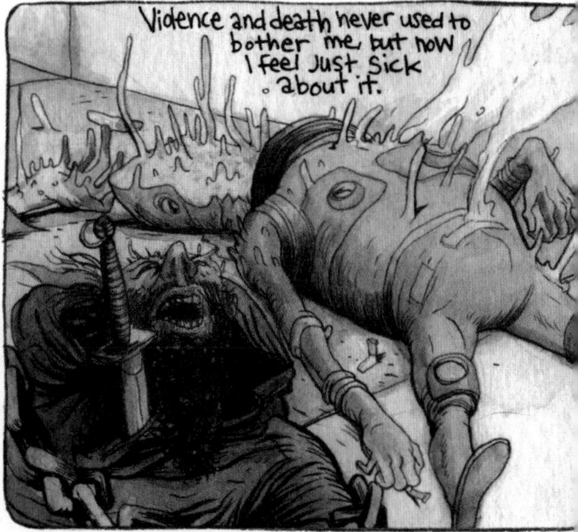

I had a weird dream.
Bance was there, and Marsi, 'cept she was a little older and...sad.

Then,
Hey, Virgil.
!
'Sup.
Sorry I didn't say hi to you last time. I was just coming down from some intense bullshit.
Aw it's cool, man. I might be gone now but we had some swell times, eh?
Gone?

Yeah, I died. Later, pal.
Bye.
Guilt, Shame.

When I was there before it lasted like a real, real long time but it wasn't bad.
I forgot that I saw young Sherwood in there too.
!
Hey, Hollis.
That place was...peace.
I didn't want to leave it. I just breathed it in.

Crow brother Thaddeaus, I know...
Is Orson. here?
My friend Sherwood was there too. He was a kid like me.
All our Sorrows.
Huh?
Stoney seems the most spiritual to me.
Hey, Sherwood.
Whoa, you can see me?
Probably due to all the drugs I take.
This is so weird, like I am watching someone elses dream.
Hey, this is my dang dream.
As soon as I thought that, I was all of a sudden back in that vortex.
?
Then I remembered...

guh.

Snif
Hollis, why are you crying?

I miss my mom so much.
Snif

Z
JAD and Sabina Spectarla were gone that morning. We never found out where they went, and Scientist just acted like nothing happened.

It's been a bunch of months or years even, and we're all real tired and depressed.
Why is nobody talking about Gun-guy?
His name was Steve.
Tad got a new buddy on the horribly long stairs.

Scientist says it is a Gnermal and that you can only see it if it chooses you to. I was real happy for Tad 'cause he needed a pal.
murp.
Snif

Because just the day before another bad thing happened.
This time it was the gun guy.

No one knew why it was happening.
Help him, guys.
?
Shit, just stay back OK, kid. Shit.
WE MUST KILL HIM.

But we didn't kill him. We all just stood there while bug-guy skittered off. Poor fella.
Shit, im so sorry. sorry.

This adventure has way too much walking, but every once in a while, total action.

SHADOWS-MEN.
THIS IS WHAT WE'VE PREPARED FOR.
Crud.
Real frikkin' Shadowsmen.
Dang.
About time.
Scientist Just zapped all of them.

The fight went on for about three hours.

The demon ninja knew what it was like to die by the hand of a Wrenchie,

But I am getting super grossed out by all this killing and death and stuff.

Scientist says that the spell he used kept us hidden from the bad guys. We killed like 720 or some such bad guys that day. We are a pretty good team eh, God?
The dead bodies got disintegrated like all magical things do here. Not like those poor little kids with hacked off faces back at the costume machine. What goes on with how this mad place works?

I Just thought of this old crazy guy who lived on my street back home. He was always cursing real loud, saying the "F" word and screaming all the time.

Mom said that when he was my age he was a preacher. But then he started hearing a devil's voice saying a real bad swear, over and over.

He tried to pray it away and pretend he didn't hear it. After a long time he went to doctors and took pills, but I guess nothing worked because he went nuts.

That devil came to me one night I think. I said "NO!" and prayed until I fell asleep.
HA, You're a weird one, Hollis.

I am weird?! How come?
It's a cool weird.
Yeah, "weird" in a real good way.

Yeah, we all really like you.
Oh, ha ha, cool.

Everyone seems to be trying so hard to stay positive but we're all super duper tired.
Yeah, We all need to use the gifts we are given.
?
God, why didn't you tell us that Gnermal was really a Gnermitamal? It got all big and scary and tried to get us.
Tad
Murmur died. He sacrificed himself.
Tad had to blow up both his old friends.
I hate this place. Nothing is good here.

You've got to know me! Look at me! Oh Daddy.

You mustn't cry. You mustn't cry. We must be good soldiers, you know.
But I have been a good soldier, Daddy!

Hey it's a TV!
And you don't know me!

Playing that old movie,
with Shirley Temple.
I love this.
Yes.
My little Sara never cries.

But I'm Sara! I'm Sara!

C'mon, Hollis!
Yes.
Yes.
Sara. Sara. My baby. My darling.
Oh, Daddy.

Scientist tells us a lot of neat stories.
THEY KEEP THE CHILDREN UNDER THE EARTH AND FORCE THEM TO OPERATE VIDEO MACHINES THAT TRANSFORM THEIR FLESH AND VERY SOULS.
Hey, how much farther is our walk gonna be?
It's hard to buy all this "EVIL" business.
?

NOW HOLLIS, REMEMBER YOU WEREN'T GOING TO ASK THAT ANYMORE.
burp.
THE DEMONIC FORCES ARE SO NUMEROUS THEY STAND SHOULDER TO SHOULDER IN OUR ATMOSPHERE.
Devils in the clouds.
woah.

Can't see it,
but I sure can feel it.
taste it, too.
So why don't we all use that vortex machine to go back and change shit.

WE CAN'T CHANGE THE PAST, GOAT. HOLLIS WENT INTO THE VORTEX AND LEFT HIS WORLD OF HIS OWN FREE WILL. TIME/SPACE IS DIFFERENT THERE.
THE AMULET ACTED LIKE A TRACTOR BEAM PULLING HOLLIS FROM THAT NEBULOUS, ENIGMATIC REALM.
SO HOLLIS, DIAMOND AND I DIDN'T TRAVEL IN TIME?

TIME/SPACE ISN'T LIKE WHAT YOU THINK IT IS. WE ARE ALL TRAVELING IN TIME ALL THE TIME.
But this isn't my earth's future, right? It's like a different dimension or something...or...
Right?

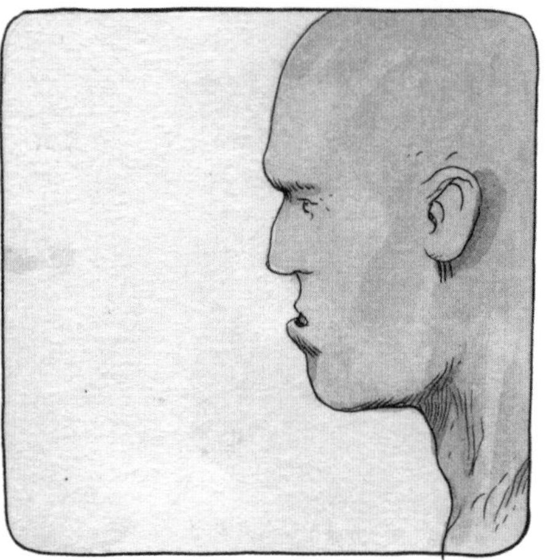

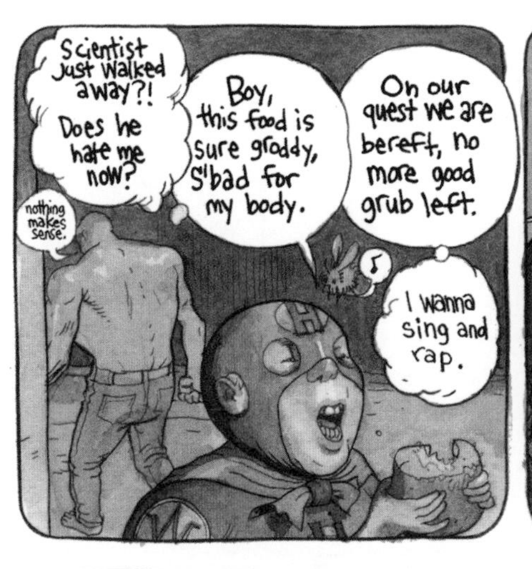
Scientist just walked away?! Does he hate me now?
nothing makes sense.
Boy, this food is sure groddy, S'bad for my body.
On our quest we are bereft, no more good grub left.
I wanna sing and rap.

Food from the Shadow's machines, scientist blessed it with his mysterious means, and now it's all cleans.
He used his special magic on the meat, made it sweet to eat.
I hope we don't all grow extra eyes and feet.

Soon we will be all out of pills Bance has the most demon kills.
I miss my mom, my bed, and my televisuals. I really love all my new pals, but am a scared by all the terrible thrills.
!
tap

CLAP CLAP CLAP CLAP CLAP CLAP CLAP CLAP CLAP

VERY GOOD, HOLLIS, THAT WAS MAGIC.
CLAP CLAP
YOU ARE RIGHT IN A WAY, THIS IS ANOTHER WORLD CRAFTED BY SHERWOOD'S HAND.
?
NOT IN THE SAME MANNER AS THE POCKET PLANE HE MADE INSIDE THE AMULET FOR DIAMOND AND GOAT.
THAT WAS A GESTATION UNIVERSE, A TRAINING GROUND THAT GAVE THEM POWER AND POTENTIAL, DEAD TO THEIR OLD FORMS AND BORN AGAIN AS MAGICAL REDEMPTION.
YEAH, Five of us "born again" Just to have three of us quick "die again."
I am so glad you quit wearing that stupid cowboy hat, Goat.
Oh, Is Sherwood a vengeful "God" or uh, whatever?
No, HE WAS A WIZARD TRYING TO PREVENT APOCALYPSE. HE JUST DIDN'T WORK FAST ENOUGH TO FIND SOMEONE ELSE TO CONJURE YOU UP.
I am the only person I know on earth that can do magic.
Should I take out an ad? Where? How?
newspaper?
tv?
website
?

Geeze, so many innocent dead for that? Sherwood was a creep.
hey, NO.
He is my friend.
No one is really pure. We are all born to sin and fall short of the glory of God. My pastor says we all deserve hell.
Ok, That is all bullshit. My mates got their freaking faces hacked off by demons.
Did they "deserve" that?
Oh. ho.
I'm sorry,
poor kids.
SHERWOOD WANTED TO DO WHAT WAS RIGHT.
EVEN NOW HIS SPIRIT IS WITH US, PRESENT, PATIENT,
STRIVING TO BRING FORTH HIS OWN AND THIS WORLD'S SALVATION.
... SUBTLY... SLOWLY...

INFLUENCING, NUDGING,
ASSISTING US IN MANY WAYS WE CAN'T SEE.
HIS BODY IS A CURSED VEHICLE FOR THE WORLD'S CORRUPTION.
OH, BUT HIS SPIRIT IS OUR SECRET ACCOMPLICE FOR THE WORLD'S RENEWEL.
WOW.
Sherwood is like a god or...
maybe WE ALL just came out of his imagination.
Do we know if our lives are real? How do we know this isn't all some dumb dream?
Bance and Marsi look a little bit older to me now...
VERY GOOD MARSI- WHAT IS REALITY? THIS COULD ALL BE A DREAM ANY ONE OF US IS EXPERIENCING, OR JUST SHERWOOD'S OWN ELABORATE DELUSION.
crack
CRACKLE
spack!

Yeah, this world doesn't make any sense, like a nightmare.
It sure isn't what I would dream up,

A feudal society, oppressed by alien demons,
Disease and violence seem bound to every molecule.
Not that our old world was all that great.
Corruption, greed, waste, and fear were all part of the human condition.

It's just so dang depressing here.
this place has it's own weird sort of melancholic beauty,
and an ambiguous purpose, and villain to rally against,
but it's getting harder and harder to see the point in anything anymore.

Does anything really matter? I'd tell you, "Do not despair," but we all have to find our own reasons for going on.

The Shadowsmen can't reproduce without our bodies. That is their fucked motivation, harvesting us to increase their numbers.
Ending their violent cycle is my motivation. We are all going on faith and our perceptions. Really look and listen and you will know the right thing to do.
We must see it to the end.
The play is the thing. The journey, not the destination. What else are we gonna do? Fighting is the only thing I'm good at.

WE ARE ALL SLOWLY PERFORMING A COSMIC DANCE. BY TAKING THIS PATH, IT IS IMPORTANT WE DO SO WITH CLEAR MINDS, FREE OF THE DELUSION OF A SELF-IDENTITY.

WE MUST NOT GET BOGGED DOWN BY THE DESPAIR, ANXIETY AND FEAR; REALIZE WE ARE THE UNIVERSE, WE ARE SPACE DUST, EVERYONE OF US PARTS OF THE EVERYTHING.

WE KNOW THIS AND WE GO ON. WE MUST GO ON
FOR OUR OWN SAKES.
FOR MY FRIEND. FOR SHERWOOD.

Hey God, Jad and Sabina Spectarla appeared unto us...
...
They are way older. Jad's tongue was all cut out now and he can't talk anymore. I think those guys are even married now too. Spectarla is super strong like Diamond is. She says they are off having their own adventures but wanted to stop by to give us some encouragement and say, "hello."
...

They were gone in the morning.

Do you all hear the geese?

We draw near to our goal.

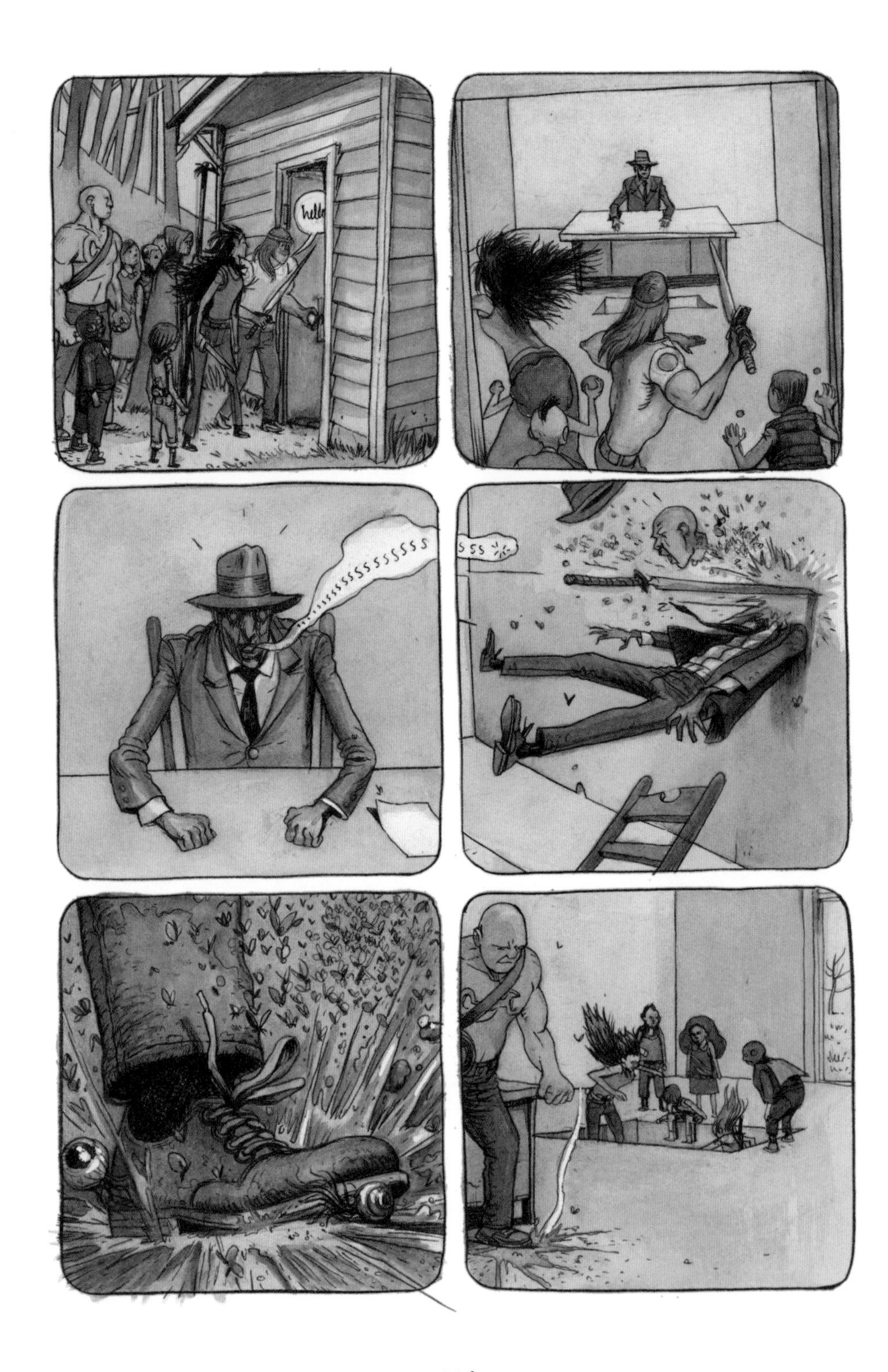
hell
ssssssssssssssssssssssss
sss

Soft.

I'm not scared.

We all went through the same door but each into our own special places.
And I could see then that we are alone.
Death comes for all of us, and we all die alone.
But I know that there is nothing to fear now.
None of the dumb things of this world matter to me.
I'm not scared. Everything is cool.

Hollis's path

In the rooms the children come and go, all their days and egos known.

In the tomb the children move slow hearing the nightmare's radio

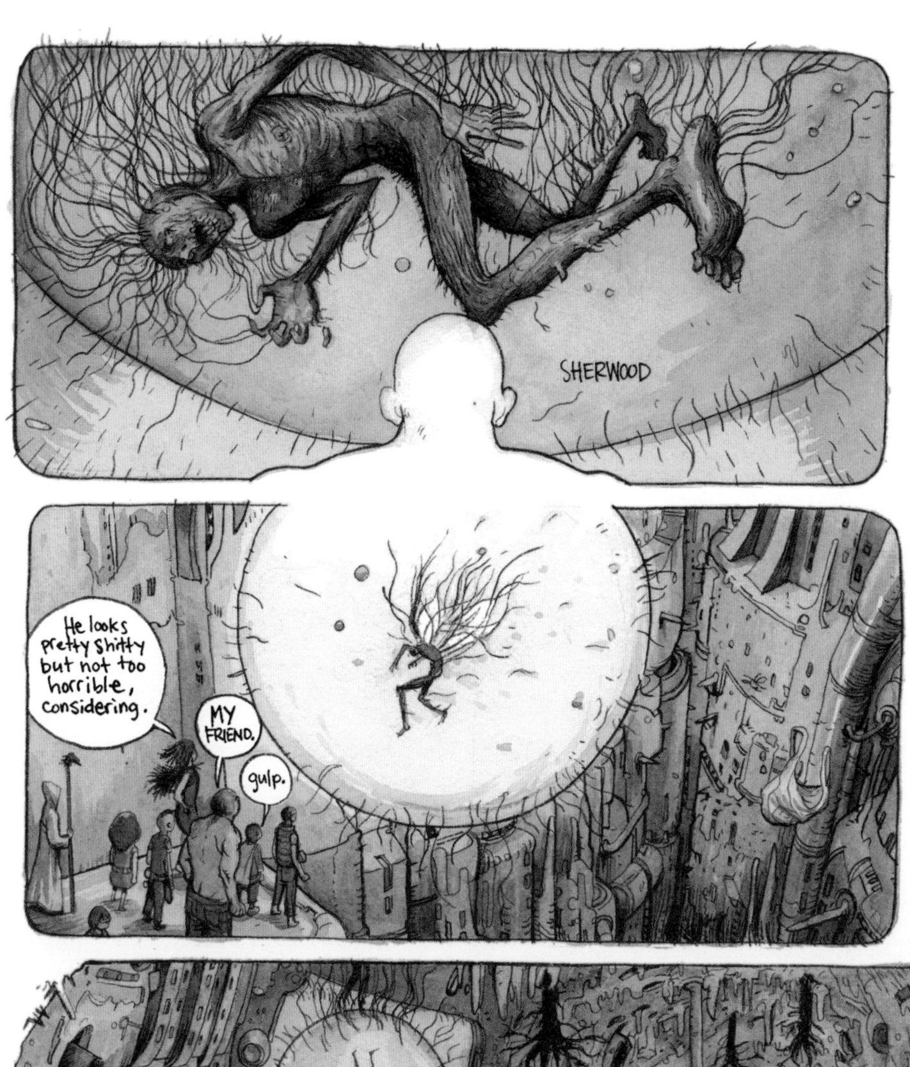
SHERWOOD
He looks pretty shitty but not too horrible, considering.
MY FRIEND.
gulp.

...

So which one of us is going to kill him?
Not me.
I can't think straight.
I... I'M AFRAID I'M UNABLE TO DO IT RIGHT NOW.
THE DESPAIR IS BREAKING THROUGH MY PROTECTIVE SPELLS. IT'S TAKING ALL MY MAGIC TO KEEP MY ROBOT BODY FROM TOTAL BREAKDOWN.
Horrid.
I feel like I've been here before.
SHADOWS HAVE GREAT POWER OVER MANY THINGS IN THIS PLACE.
How long have we all been standing here?
LOOK! THEY STIR. THEY RISE.
WE NEED TO QUICKLY PERFORM OUR TASK. THE SHADOWSMEN WILL BE ON US SOON.
Task? Oh yeah, I forgot.
And what do we do after we kill the guy?
I feel real bad about all this crud.

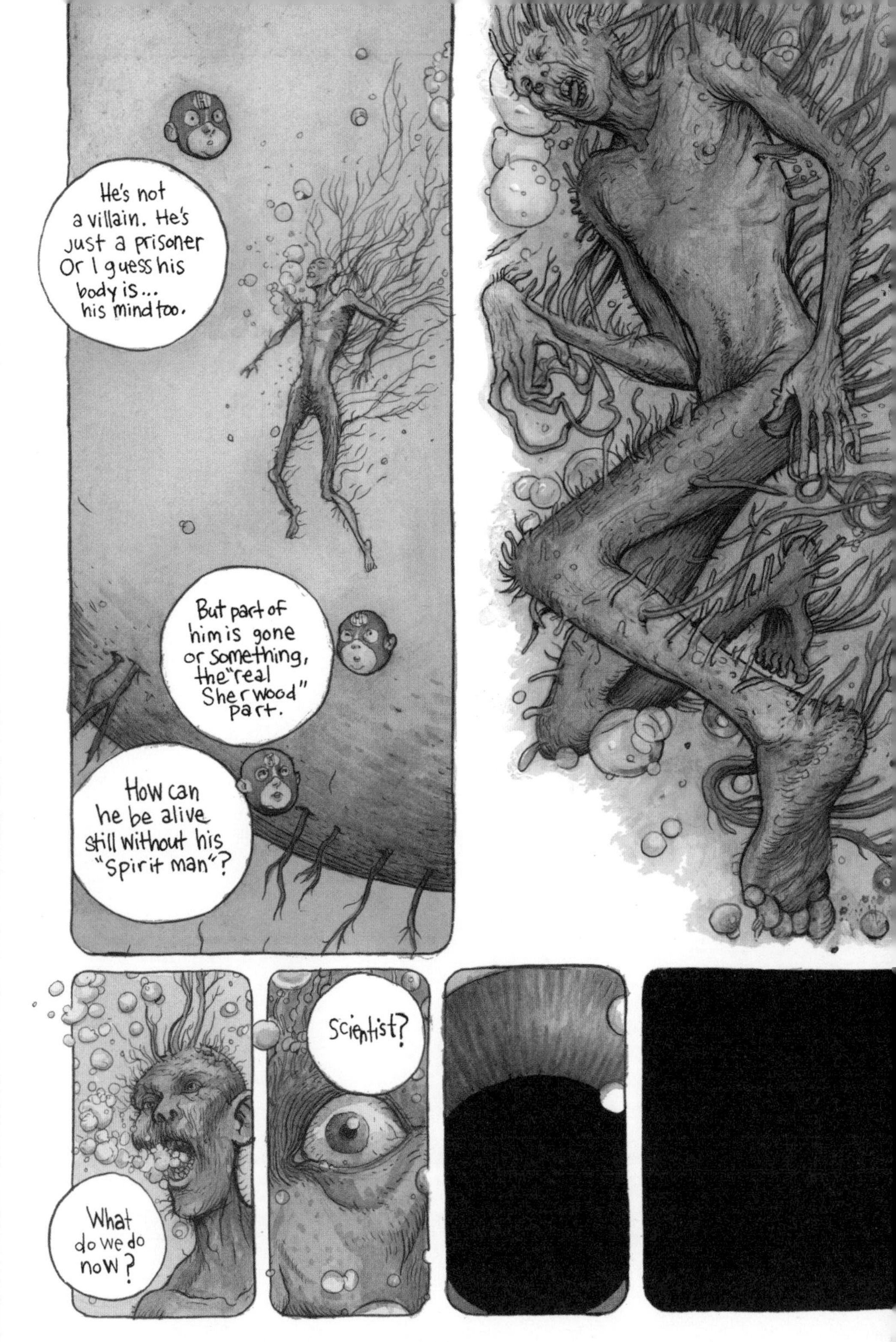
He's not a villain. He's just a prisoner Or I guess his body is... his mind too.
But part of him is gone or something, the "real Sherwood" part.
How can he be alive still without his "spirit man"?
What do we do now?
Scientist?

Chapter 6
Sherwood Presley Breadcoat

It's so big here.

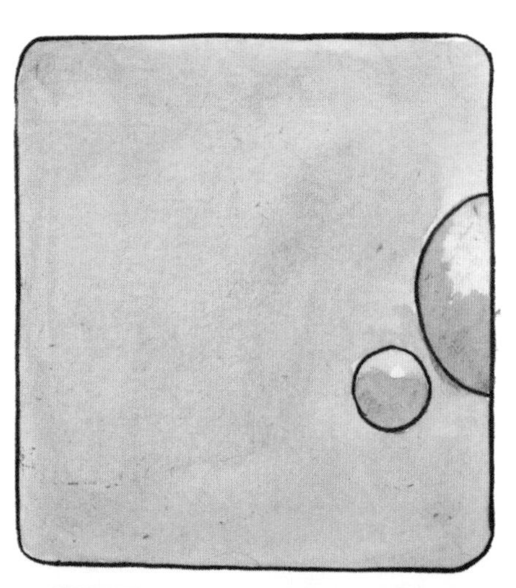

It never ends.

Bubbles of thought ... or memory
surrounded by ... nothing.

My past, my future, All things known now.

No, nothing known now.

know

nothing

this one
I think.

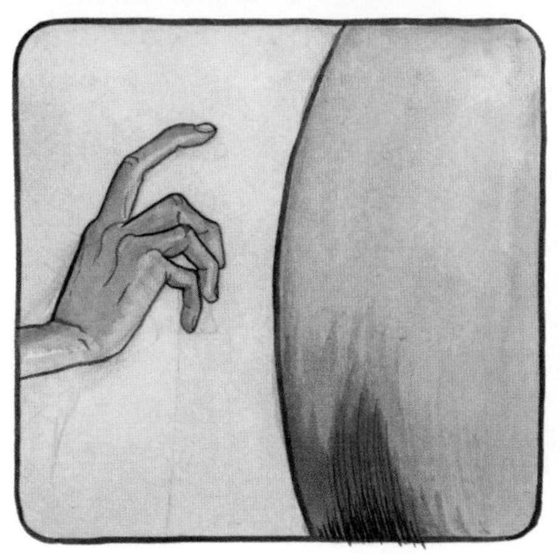

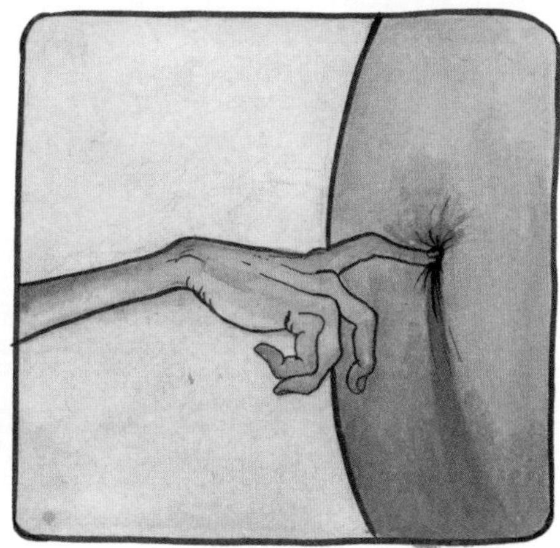

This is Sherwood.
Thirty-Five years old, No phone. No car.

Narcissist. Drug Addict.

Sherwood has spent most of his life fighting demonic entities he calls Shadowsmen.

Fortune Sceptre, Sherwood's best pal:
I remind him of Orson.
He told me so.

Marsi Parasol,
girlfriend?
Alter-ego?
Not really.

Sherwood's boss:
Sherwood is such a natural.

Notice his resemblance to the dark elf from that cave.
THE CAVE.

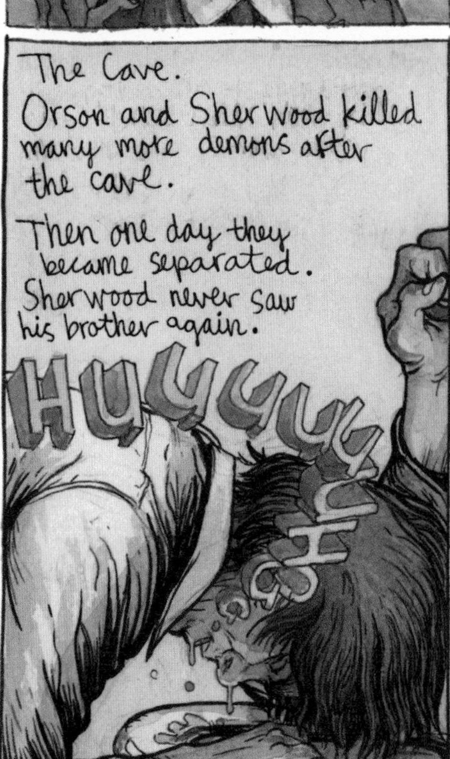
The Cave.
Orson and Sherwood killed many more demons after the cave.
Then one day they became separated. Sherwood never saw his brother again.
HUUUUU
GH

Now he thinks too much about how he used to feel before his life as an adventurer.
Everything felt so weird back then. Was it the same for every kid?
Blurrgh
Fuuuck.

Much of his adolescence was spent in another reality. Since returning to earth Sherwood has found relating to most people very difficult.

Why am I such a dick? Fuck!

Shit! Damn. I suck.

I really need to stop wasting so much fucking water.

His day job as a remote viewer could seem exotic to an outsider.
...nd I suddenly see myself as this total jerk.
mmm
So tired of this shit.
Sherwood practices magic to help control his growing neurosis.

?

Shit. ohmygod. No.
no.

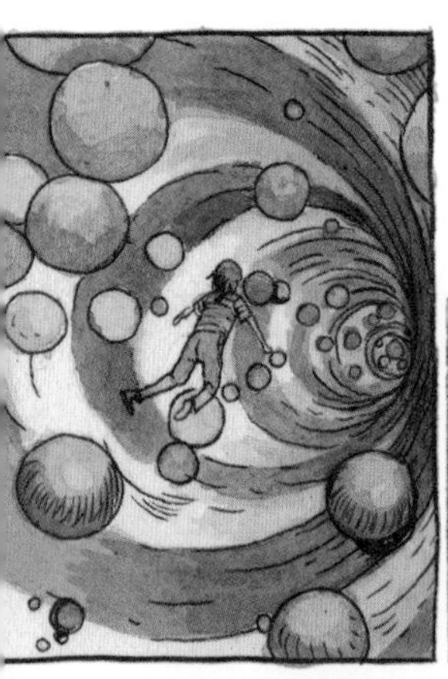

I lost my mom.
Lost my brother.
Everything.
Each bubble...

Sherwood; hobo / drifter / adventurer / demon slayer.
Always Looking For Orson
always.
five years wandering
age 28-33

Then at age 33

Sherwood sees and remembers something
oh no.

Age 35 Sell out government spook.

It is all so I can look for Orson.

Occasionally he kills a demon or three.

Sherwood feels bad all the time

gah
Before the cave Sherwood and most other children he knew were raised with some sort of religion.
After the cave all of that seemed sort of silly to Sherwood and his brother.

Much of what people told Sherwood as a child went against his natural intuition.
I'm just trying to figure out why I believe in anything now.
Shhhh. Not now.
YOU KNOW THAT THERE IS MORE TO BOTH OUR WORLDS THAN THE VISIBLE SPECTRUM,
BUT I FIND THAT MOST DO NOT WANT TO HEAR ABOUT THAT.
Indeed! Earth's moon is quite hollow. It's a space-ship.
So is Phobos of Mars.
Booze and drugs numb me. The amulet focuses my magical energy. But I still...
Man, you are way too identified with your mental formations.
We all know the world is super fucked but what can we do?
Don't you meditate every day? You should.
Sherwood started working as a government agent to look for his brother. Now he can't think of why that seemed a good reason.
!
I need to snap out of this!
Maybe I should kill my boss?
I feel like crying all day at work.
Then I get furious when my boss asks me,
What's wrong, son?

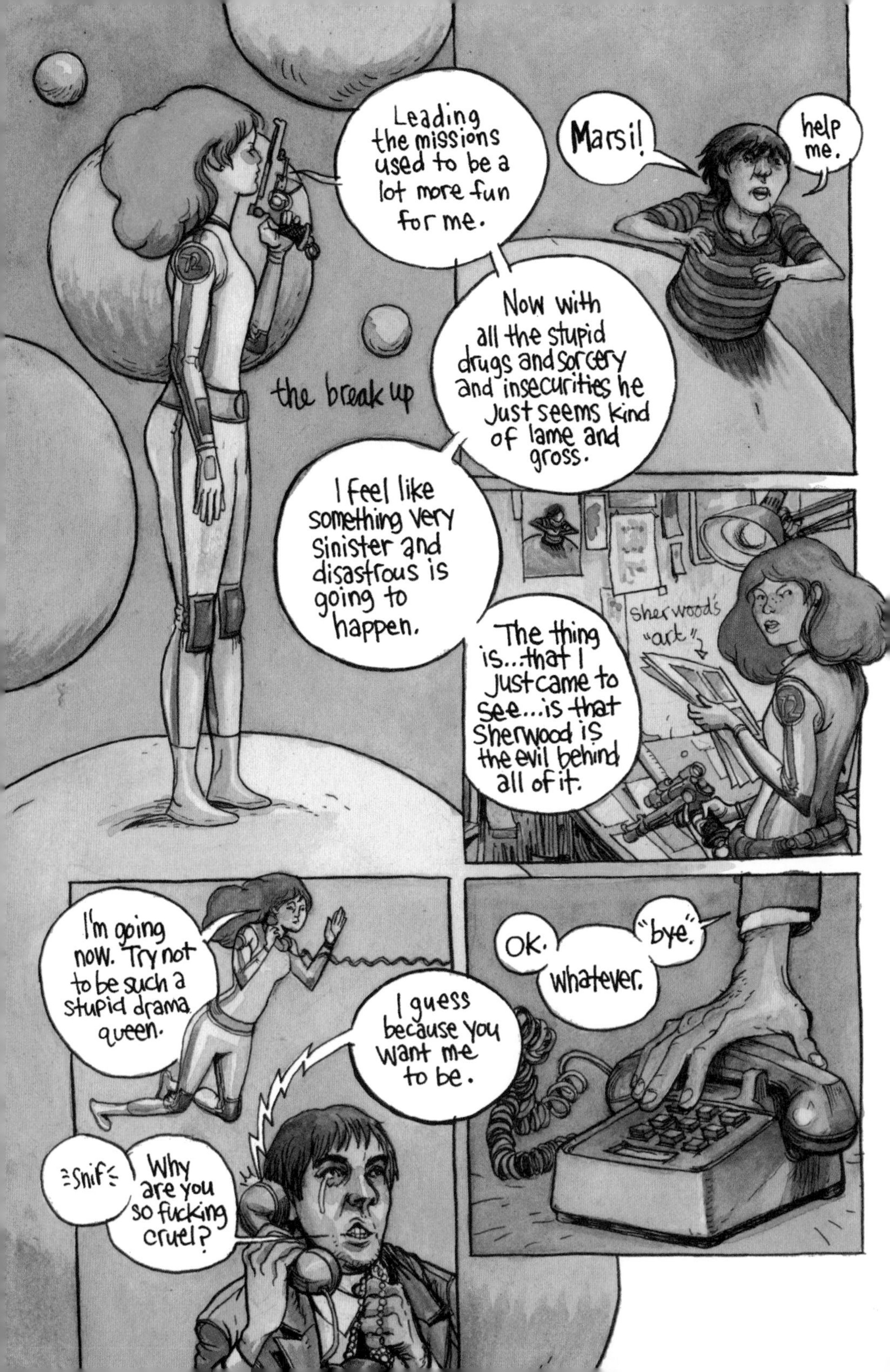
the break up
Leading the missions used to be a lot more fun for me.
Now with all the stupid drugs and sorcery and insecurities he just seems kind of lame and gross.
I feel like something very sinister and disastrous is going to happen.
Marsi!
help me.
sherwood's "art"
The thing is...that I just came to see...is that Sherwood is the evil behind all of it.
I'm going now. Try not to be such a stupid drama queen.
I guess because you want me to be.
snif
Why are you so fucking cruel?
OK.
whatever.
"bye."

The demons won't stop coming. Sherwood used to enjoy the struggle.
The ego feeding off your inner turmoil defines the mental picture you have of yourself.
So, can anyone else see these, "demons"?
I don't know, just me and Orson, I guess.

Listen.
Oh no.
Oh God, I'm so sorry for all the shitty things I've done and people I've hurt.
You are just suffering from a world view passed on to you by your parents.
Yeah, I do relate a lot to this dorky fat kid who lives next to me.
His mom's pretty religious like my mom was.

Except the big difference between me and him is that he dresses up like a superhero, while I actually was one sort of.

ha ha.
snort

Wait! Should we really be doing this?
I mean... Shit.
Maybe you're right.
You wanna just do more blowcaine powder?

Going in there felt a bit like waking up hungover and next to a dirty ashtray.

Orson was usually better at most things.

I called the caves, "The crazy station" because walking into one was like nothing you felt before, even in dreams!
It is sort of like a real intense mush-room trip.
Wow, you talk like all that shit is for real. It sounds so goddamn nuts. That must be why we are pallies.

Fortune doesn't believe in Sherwood.
You broke into my home and killed my slave giant.
After I use your own blade to carve up your little neck,
Not again;
Where are you, Orson?
The city is bleeding.
The rats are fleeing.
The locust despair.

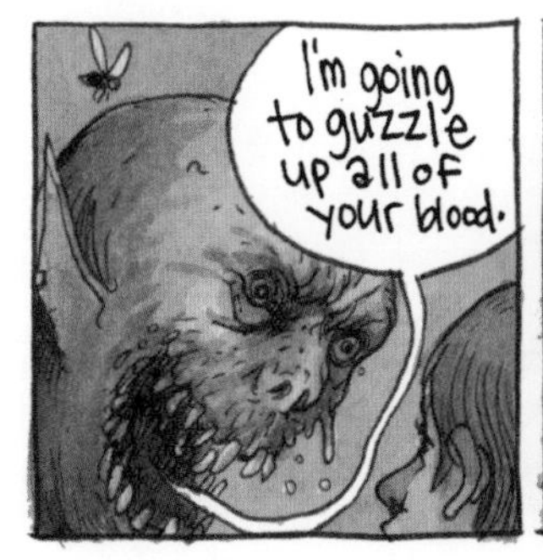
I'm going to guzzle up all of your blood.

Ohhh, you are so afraid, boy.

HA! YES!

IT'S AWESOME! HAHA!
Shut up.
fuck you!
HA HA HA HA!
Smack
Stab.-

Sherwood.
I was afraid.

Sorry I'm so dang late.
S'okay. Just killed another one.

hurrrk.

Ha hah! You puked, sucker!
Yeah.

It was just 'cause of that groddy smell.
I'm used to it now.

I'm used to it now.
the Emilie

Meanwhile in the past or future somewhere...

On board the Proxima Centauri.
The spaceship, as big as several of the major cities on earth is where Sherwood first meets Marsi.
The day Sherwood turns 15 he finally sees his opportunity.
The time traveler helps his escape,
GOOD BYE.
but forgets to tell Sherwood that he knows exactly where his brother Orson is.

Back on earth.

Sherwood, on the same evening, goes out on his first date and is transformed by music for the first time.
huh?
He is sixteen years old.
WOW.
One of the biggest regrets in his life is leaving that show without saying goodbye to Emily.
Amulet says there's a demon.
Outside the club Sherwood keeps thinking the future will be better.
Also for the first time he wonders if the demons will ever stop coming.
Worms!?
Jesus!
Fuck!

I am really just part of you, dummy.
I'm also another type of energy.
Hey, are you high right now?
Oh
uh
yeah.

Is that bad?
Whatever, I'm not your mother.

ha hah yeah, I know.

Oh, God.
What a creep and an asshole.

Oh Shit! Did I Just say all that out loud?
Hey, is that guy a Shadowsman? Nah, he's way too big.
Oh.
WOW.
She looks like-
Uh-oh
Shit.
Damn.
Why did I look away and didn't even smile? God, I'm a weirdo.

Sherwood meets Marsi on the astral plane.

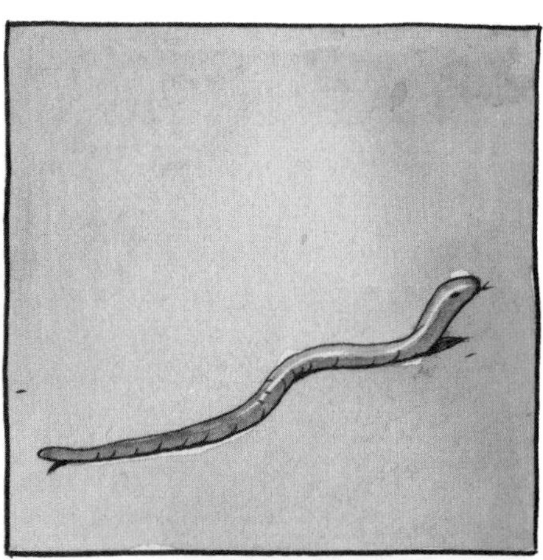

The protective spells around Sherwood's apartment begin to weaken because of all the time he spends feeding his own concept of pain.

Let's not make a big deal about this but I fucking resign.
?!
Wait.
This is wrong.
It's bullshit.

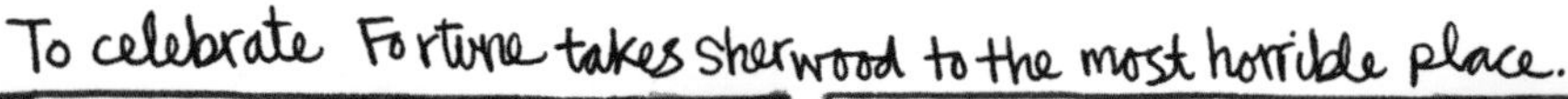
To celebrate Fortune takes Sherwood to the most horrible place.

Uh... heh heh, that's a joke?
Not laughing am I, fucker?
No, but I thought you might have a dry sense of humor. You're threatening me, for real?
Oh, I am most assuradly threatening you.
So, like, you are gonna physically try to harm me... with violence?
Something along those lines.
oh.

I cried about that for three days. God, never in my youth did I think I would do something like that. What if I had killed that kid?
Whatever, he was wearing the uniform of a bastard.
Don't you ever get "The Shame"?
No way, man. I am legend.
Sometimes my life feels like this undramatic lame re-enactment.

You want to rob a fucking bank with me?
All right, but why not just raid one of your, "elf caves"?

I don't go into caves anymore.

Jesus, I really have no clue what I'm doing.

Nobody does. Some of us are just better at faking it.

Coming back from the bank job.

A constant fear of Sherwood's is that he will grow up to be the world's ultimate evil.
If you hold still they nibble on your legs.

ha
ha
hah
tickles
Ha ha, I remember that.
Why does older me care so much?
minnows
The next bubble shows him his worse fear made true.

No!
It's because of me.
I've got to fix it!

Instead of just passing through I'll try riding along the edge until I come to the right-

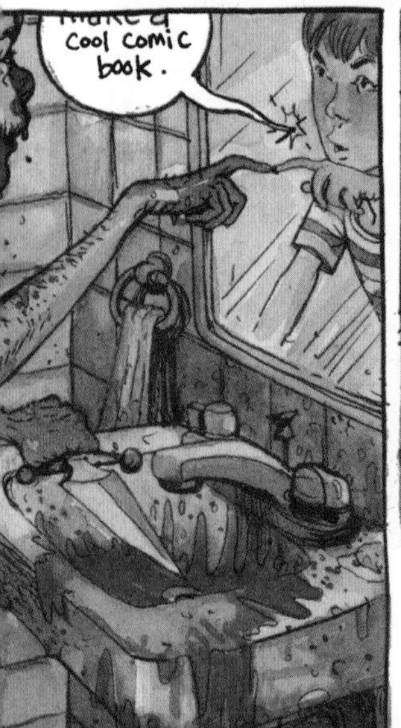
cool comic book.

Shouldn't I just kill myself?
cut

I HAVE always wanted to make a comic book.

N
N
N
Please, Sherwood. Stay with us.

Rot and filth inside,

and they go creeping.

creak
There is no joy, only weeping.

All right, crawly!

Freakin' dang dammit!

Making comic books can be sort of like killing dark elves. Die, bastards.
You are doing great, son.
Thanks, brother Thaddeaus.

Secret tesseract engine room
Sherwood doesn't leave his apartment for months that feel like years.

The only way you are getting that finished is if you never see anyone.
The amulet will get me through.
We miss you buddy.

I'm just trying to make sense of all this. How can I say... Just enough?
Sincerity and subtlety infused with sorcery.
Hmm, maybe you should make a movie or a music album to get your "secret message" out?
Cool. I'm like a real comic book artist.
No offense you guys, but I'm putting my head phones on for a while.

Finally...
The Wrenchie's
1st ISSUE
Ms. M. Parasol
Why'd you call it that?
And Super-heroes? That Shit's kind of played — no offense.
Yeah, I guess it sucks but I needed to do it. I had to cast the spell and find a conjurer.
Weird. Isn't there just some sort of underground wizard network?
Not really.
And book orders were pretty low too.
Look man, I think you are a decent artist but... this is just not my thing.
I don't really get it.
Let's get fucked up!
Meanwhile, somewhere else.
oh.
Unfortunately the wizard was taken out by shadowsmen.
I need to contact this person, fast!

Astral projection

Holy fuck. Almost blocked from getting back in.
I am such a stupid prick.
I'm Just an asshole paying for all the horrible things I've done.
All the mean words,
mental judgments,
killing those high school kids.
!
:huf: How did :huf: they get in my apartment? :huf:
Amulet's supposed to protect my home. :huf:
Maybe you should make a comic about it?
Wanna do more drugs?
Nah,
but get the fuck out of here.

Sherwood did not think his plan through very well.

Blackout drunk for the last time.

The next day, hungover for the last time.

I can't remember.

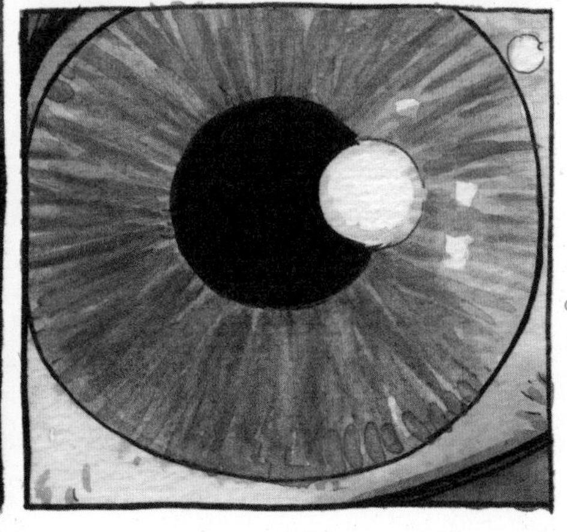

I AM SORRY, HOLLIS. THE SHIELD IS UNSTABLE.
I CAN'T MOVE.
no.
I know what to do.
I read it in the Wrenchies comic.
I can do it.

Here you go, Sherwood.

MY STRENGTH RETURNS,
AND MOST OF THE DEMONS RETURN TO THE DUST. AND ASH.
hurk
ew.
EVEN NOW THEIR EVIL POWER IS DIMINISHING.
KOF

Hollis.
gulp.
I can remember all of it.
cough
here you go, sir.
All of those lives destroyed, all the suffering, the devestation.
They needed my body. they used me to power their nightmare devices.
So only one of my Wrenchies made it here, eh?
It was enough I guess-kof kaf
The Spell worked it out eventually.
I kaf- I should have planned it better, should have stopped it sooner.
I kind of remember you now.

You are the real hero, Hollis, the one I was supposed to be- ≷cough≶.
I just saw too much.
After a while it all seemed so boring and stupid.
My life was ≷heh≶ adventure, then a joke, then an insane and very long dream. ≷gasp≶
The world was cast into bondage because of me. ≷wheeze≶
Evil powered by my everlasting nightmare. ≷sob.≶
?
YES, SHERWOOD, BUT NOW THE NIGHTMARE IS COMING TO AN END AND THE PLANET HAS A CHANCE TO HEAL ITSELF.
After Sherwood's gone are we all gonna still exist?
Oh yes.
We are.
?
The world's still screwed up but at least we get to kill this guy.

Sherwood dies apologizing

the end.

Epilogue: Hollis and the Scientist wrap it up.

I think Stoney, Marsi, and Diamond all travel around the galaxy together in a space ship/time machine.

Tad sat for a while until he had a good idea.

Later on some of us will be space rocket jet pilots.
Orson
Hollis
Bance
Tad
Shakey
Smith

Before all of that though I spend some time going around on this weird airship thing.

Oh, yeah, and the scientist rests for a long time.
He's real old.
...

Epilogue 2: The Amulet through time and space,

hey, Belf.

Did you see that?

No, I was watching one of those nephalim ships.
Look.

this weird thing just appeared.
I wouldn't touch that, rat.

I like it.
mine.
ok.
Rub it all over your face if you want.

Hey, maybe we should crash that kid's party later?
Solid, I got a feeling Shadowsmen will show up.

Epilogue 3: Back to Sherwood and Orson in the cave.

We'll just have to kill all of them.
Yeah, we'll get all those creeps.

We just need to get out of this cave before I throw up.

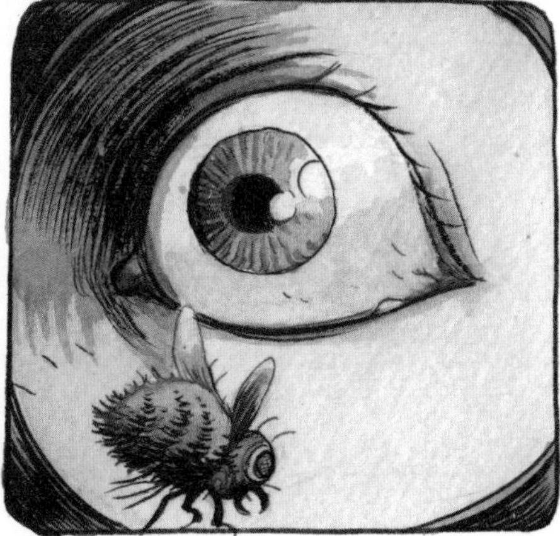

Epilogue 4: Sherwood and Marsi on the astral plane again.

thank you: Valerie Dickie, Sandra McVicker, Krista Dalrymple, Sarah Palmer, Bernadette Baker-Baughman, Mark Siegel, Gina Gagliano, Calista Brill, Colleen Venable, Zachary Baldus, Zack Soto, Andrew Carl, Chris Stevens, Locust Moon, Josh O'Neill, Craig Thompson, Greg Means, MK Reed, Jason Sacher, Katya Amato, Diana Schutz, Bob Schreck, Rick Remender, Danni Remender, Gabriel Taylor, Tom Taylor, Alex Cahill, Andy Bodor, Andy Johnson, Adam Healy, Annie Nocenti, Jason Leivian, Brandon Graham, Brian Scott O'keefe and the Keefe family, Bruce Waldman, Chris Lutes, Chris McDonnell, Chris Pitzer, Brett Warnock, Dan Zalkus, Matt Dicke, Douglas Sherwood, Jasen Lex, Esao Andrews, Fernando Fuentes, Nancy Bishop, Fred Espinosa, Henry Covey, Gretchen Stelter, Hannes Ludwig, Helen Popinchalk, Indigo Kelleigh, James Jean, Jeff Mason, Jeffrey Brown, Jennie Yim, Jennifer Parks, Jim Campbell, Sean Christensen, Joe Flood, Joel Meadows, Joey William Belden, John Greiner, Johnny Granado, Jon Palmer, Jonathan Hickman, Joshua Dysart, Ryan Alexander-Tanner, Jonathan Lethem, Jordan Crane, Jose Villarrubia, Joseph Bergin III, Joseph Cross, Jody LeHeup, Molly Lazer, Aubrey Sitterson, Thomas Brennan, Jennifer Grunwald, Kathleen Garrity, Keith Mayerson, Kieron Dwyer, Casey Farnum, Nate Powell, Mike Lirely, Leland Purvis, Leonard Wong, Liam Baranauskas, Jungle Ben Cady, Marc Clapham, Markland Starkie, Martin French, Mary Gibbons, Matthew Southworth, Michael Drivas, Amir Malekpour, Mike Mignola, Jeff Smith, Morgan Dontanville, Mu Wen Pan, Nicholas Gazin, Nicole Schneit, Multnomah County Library, Paul Hornschemeier, Paul Pope, Peter Birkemoe, Christopher Butcher, Peter Laird, Raffaele Timarchi, Rafer Roberts, Regino Gonzales, Reid Psaltis, Matthew Ocasio, Rico Renzi, Rob G, Rob Casteel, Gillian Robespierre, Rob Stolzer, Rob Vollmar, Robin McConnell, Roger Peffley, S.W. Conser, Michael and Sally Sue Lander, Sam Liberto, Sammy Harkham, Sarah Orner, Scott Mills, Seamus Heffernan, Serge Marcos, Shannon Stewart, Shawna Gore, Sierra Hahn, Simon Roy, Stephanie Czerniewski, Steve Halker, Jamie Pierson, Corey Petit, Stuart Geddes, Theo Ellsworth, Thomas Herpich, Tim Goodyear, Tim Hamilton, Todd Bak, Tom Brevoort, Tom Neely, Tomer and Asaf Hanuka, François Vigneault, Tristan Yuhas, Troy Zeigler, Wallace McBride, Walt Parrish, Walter Simonson, Louise Simonson, Valter Guevarra, Warren Bernard, Wendy Chin, George Hage, Vincent Stall, Jeff Kilpatrick, Amanda Rothstein, Margaret Liss, Naomi Hospodarsky, Lisa Dennis, Edward Bignar, William Burkert, Robin Bougie, Joo Chung, John Fantastic, Ivan Sleeper III, Kyle Loffelmacher, Bwana Spoons, Jad Ziade, Alex Cox, Anthony Alvarado, Steven Parke, Garret Izumi, Richard Miller, Meathaüs, Lucas May, Tom Woodruff, Matt Hawkins, Jonny Tennant, Claire Gibson, Marian Churchland, Karen Wilke, David Galvan, Arthur Smid, Ben Kahn, Sid Scott, John Ruggeri, Bob Fingerman, Laura Hartrich, Stephen Eidson, Chris Hedges, Robert Pollard, Eckhart Tolle, Electric Wizard, Yob, David Lynch, Werner Herzog, Wes Anderson, Tim Hunter, Joe Morris, Aaron Meyers, Timothy Callahan, Mitchel Hickman, Naomi Hospodarsky, Brooke Devine, Bayard Baudoin, and all of you for reading this.

fotogloctica
by farel dalrymple

another one.

hhsssssssssssss

-hssss?

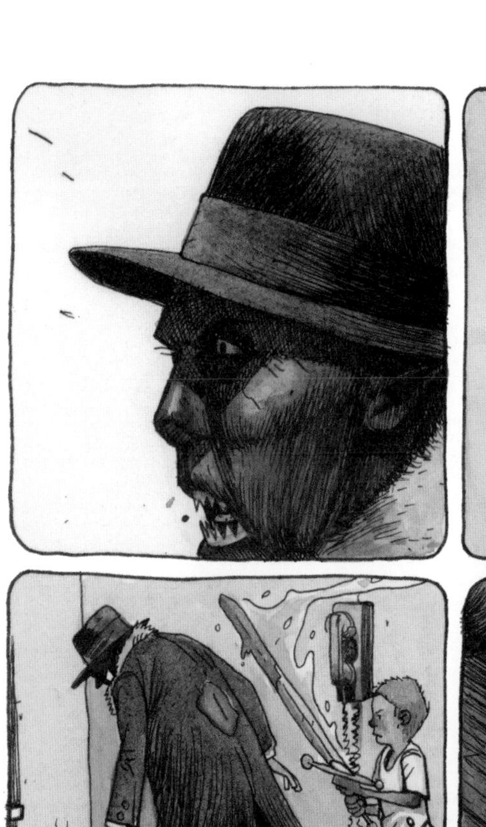

s s ssss

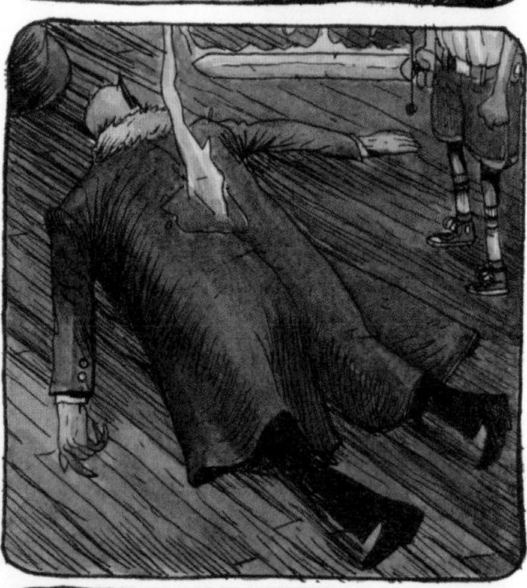

another one.

ring
ring
ring
ring
ring

ring
ring

hullo?
yep. It's done, bro.

Cool.
Decent Job, Orson.
eh, It wasn't too hard.
left some gold though.

You stabbed it in the back eh?

About a half century ago in the American Midwest...
Ha!
ow! you... you...
fucking fart head
what?! you... swore! you're in trouble.
bitch.
shut up or I'll...
no.
fuck
you!
ooooofff.
butt head.
freaking stop cussing.

hey look
c'mon.
OW.
knock it off.
poc
scratch scratch
itchy.
Whoa.
cool.
what's that?
Look!
I see it.

oh my stink.
HOLY FUCK!
Cut it out!
OW
Who
is
here?
AAAUGHH!!

hhSSSSSSSSSSSSS SSS S SSSS!
LET 'EM GO!
My eyes!
ow.
no,
Mom,
it hurts.
Oh my God ... I'm blind!
No!
hhisssssssss
CRIPES!

hhhSSS SSSSSSS
you Jerk... Stop Stealing my eyes.

ssss=,urk.
SLice
huh?

I can see.

SPONTANEOUS COMBUSTION!

whoa.

later...
I'm gonna call my sword, "shadows slayer."
yeah,... that's a cool sword...
?
ORSON, LOOK...
...What I... ...found.
I know These creatures now...
Oh shit, Orson
They know us.

They felt what happened when you killed this one.
Then let's get out of this ding-a-ling cave, Sherwood. I'm scared something bad will happen to Mom.
It's too late for Mom, Orson. Time acts funny in here. At least thirty years have passed since we first stepped into this cave. We never should have walked into this dark place...
No, brother, we can never go home again.
No.
Mom.
snif
But, we should grab whatever we can carry with us and go somewhere else. There are places in the world we can hide from them.
Let me see that thing.
No, Orson, It only works with me now.
Something that guy did to my eyes... I can see things, Orson. See things.
You see, that elf was blind, and was trying to take my eyes to use. Someone left a back door to this other realm open, and we stumbled in...
Now these evil things are coming for us.
No.
We will just kill all of THEM, first.
WE ARE COMING FOR THEM!
Mom is dead.

Let's outfit ourselves.

Then take on the dark elves.

Sherwood emerges in a future tale as an adult working as a spy with the codename "Ms. Umbrella."

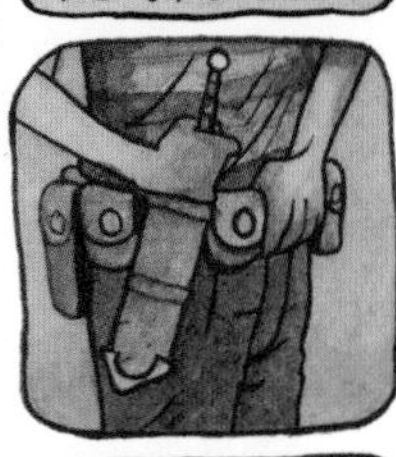

Hundreds of years later he redeems himself and all of mankind. Humanity is free and stronger than before.

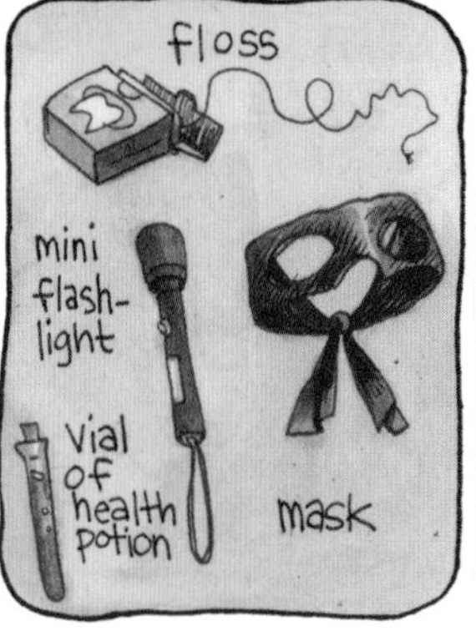

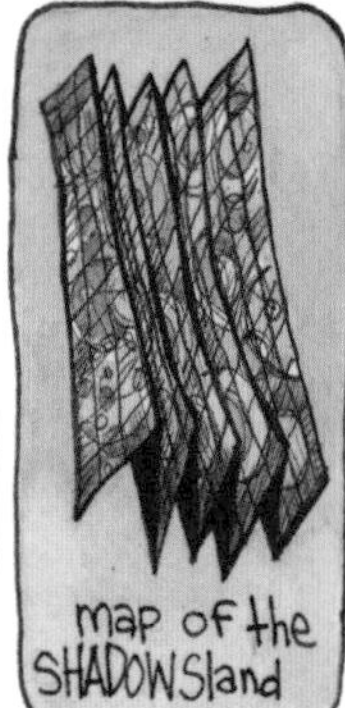

Orson killed hundreds of demons with his brother.
Orson
breadcoat
Yeah, take on the dark elves,
Mom sure would have been happy about me getting to chop demons to pieces.
pirate eyepatch
We'll kill them in sixes and twelves.
She was always telling me, "The Devil is trying to destroy your life."
gold and Jewels
After Sherwoods mysterious disappearance Orson lives in a half dream state...
I got to look after Sherwood, He's not as tough as me. He didn't even do anything when I hit him with that rock.
utility belt
Shadows slayer
(Orson at the exact moment his brother vanishes.)
Sherw....
...flying in an airship with his best buddy, Smith.
spy camera
matchbook
Aviator Sunglasses
Yo-Yo
Pocket watch
flash light
Chewing gum
POCKET KNIFE
tape measure
handkerchief
Occasionally he thinks about his brother and mother.

That's weird.

My body has returned to dust,
While my head remains intact and functional.

Hello, In case you couldn't tell, I am from a dark, dangerous, and supernatural race.
Though our name has been unknown to mortals since the ancient times,
The ignorant and the foolhardy, have referred to us as "the Shadowsmen."

But we are not men. We are...
oh.

Oh... okay... Look, here I go now. ...a little late.
All of these treasures...lost,

...In the hands of those two crazy brats.
Okay, Orson, let's get out of here.
The end.

Published by First Second
First Second is an imprint of Roaring Brook Press, a division of
Holtzbrinck Publishing Holdings Limited Partnership
175 Fifth Avenue, New York, New York 10010

Cataloging-in-Publication Data is on file at the Library of Congress.

ISBN 978-1-59643-421-9

First Second books may be purchased for business or promotional use. For information on bulk purchases please contact Macmillan Corporate and Premium Sales Department at (800) 221-7945 x5442 or by email at specialmarkets@macmillan.com.

First edition 2014
Book design by Colleen AF Venable

Printed in China

10 9 8 7 6 5 4 3